LANDRY'S BACK
IN TOWN

MARGERY SCOTT

Landry's Back in Town

This is a work of fiction. Names, characters, places and incidents are the product of the author's imagination or are used fictitiously. Any resemblance to actual persons, living or dead, events or locales is entirely coincidental.

No part of this book may be used or reproduced in any manner whatsoever without written permission of the author except in the case of brief quotations embodied in critical articles and reviews.

Books by Margery Scott

Historical romance
Emma's Wish
Wild Wyoming Wind

The Morgans of Rocky Ridge
Cade
Trey
Zane
Will
Jesse
Brett
Heath

Rose: Bride of Colorado

Rocky Ridge Romance
Landry's Back in Town
Substitute Bride
Wanted: The Perfect Husband
Hannah's Hero
High Stakes Bride

Brides of Beckham
Mail-Order Miranda
Mail-Order Melanie

Contemporary romance
Winterlude

Romantic suspense
Devil's Harvest
Out of Time
The Next Victim
Her Rocky Mountain Guardian

Medical romance
The Surgeon's Homecoming
Stranded with the Surgeon
The Firefighter and the Lady Doc

Chapter One

"Well, hello there, darlin'. Ain't you a pretty little thing?"

The slurred voice startled Olivia Harding from her reverie. Her gaze darted around, noticing for the first time that she was completely alone. Late afternoon sun cast shadows on the deserted street, and a shaft of light already spilled from the doorway of The Lucky Shamrock Saloon a few buildings away.

She'd made the ten-minute walk between her house and the Rocky Ridge Children's Home countless times over the past few months without giving any thought to her surroundings.

Until now.

She couldn't see anyone, but she wasn't the kind of woman who let her imagination run wild. Someone was lurking in the shadows.

Tendrils of fear snaked up her spine at the suggestive tone of the man's voice. Her heartbeat skittered in her chest, and a cold chill washed over her.

Suddenly, a man appeared out of the shadows between two boarded-up buildings and stood directly in her path. Foul odors assaulted her nose - liquor, cigar smoke and perspiration.

Dark hair hung in oily strings from beneath a

stained hat hanging low over his bloodshot eyes.

"Excuse me, sir," she said, doing her best to keep her voice steady. She made a move to go around him.

He blocked her path and moved toward her, his gait a little wobbly. "What's the hurry, darlin'?"

She could scream, she supposed. But who would hear her? Her cries for help would be drowned out by the voices and the music from the piano in the saloon.

She backed up a few steps, widening the gap between them. The man advanced.

She tried to sidestep him. "Let me pass. Now."

"Don't be like that, darlin'," he said, mirroring her moves while closing the gap between them to stand within a few inches of her.

Panic threatened to overwhelm her, but she took in a deep calming breath. Surely the man wanted to rob her, nothing more. "If it's money you want, take it." She shoved her embroidered reticule into the man's chest.

He laughed, grabbed the bag and tossed it aside. It landed in a pile of trash near the alley entrance. Then he threw the cigar in his hand onto the dirt street. "You got something I want far more than a few coins."

Moving much faster than she thought him capable of, he gripped her arm. She let out a shriek as he spun her around, wrapping his arm around her throat.

Terror spiked her heart rate at the thought of what he was going to do to her. She kicked and twisted, trying to land a blow to his shin, but he held fast. She clawed at his arm, but it did no good. She felt herself being half-lifted, half-dragged into the shadows between the buildings.

His arm tightened around her neck, cutting off her air. "It'll be a lot easier on you if you stop fighting," he hissed.

Dizziness washed over her. Her body weakened from the struggle to draw in a breath. Her lungs burned. Still, she couldn't give in. Some things were worse than dying.

Suddenly, she heard him grunt. Her body jerked.

Her attacker let out a guttural curse and a moment later, the pressure of his arm around her neck disappeared. Stumbling away from him, she reached out until she came into contact with the rough wood of one of the buildings.

Gasping for air, she spun around and plastered herself against the wall as she peered into the darkness. Her eyes widened as she watched her attacker and another man grappling with each other. Fists connected with flesh, neither man gaining an advantage until the stranger landed a punch to her attacker's face. Blood spurted from his nose, and she thought she heard a bone crack.

Her attacker fell backward into the dirt. Kicking out, he hooked his foot around her rescuer's ankle and jerked, knocking him off balance. He crashed into a bin beside the wall and rolled to the ground as her attacker scrambled to his feet and raced away, disappearing around the corner onto the street.

Olivia was shaking violently, while at the same time relief washed over her as her rescuer slowly got to his feet and limped toward her.

He studied her, his eyes searching her face. "Are you all right?"

"I think so." Her mouth was so dry her voice was little more than a squeak. "I ... thank you ..."

"You're sure?"

She nodded. Her throat tightened and her eyes stung. Tears threatened, which was silly. The danger was over. What did she have to cry about now? "How did you know ...? I mean, I didn't see anyone on the street."

"I was doing a job for Martin Raye."

"The undertaker?"

He nodded. "I happened to be outside when I heard a scuffle. Didn't realize what was going on until I came around the corner."

"I'm so glad you heard it," she said, her voice growing thready as the memory of her attacker's hands on her flooded her brain again. "I can't even imagine ... what might have happened if you hadn't been there. You quite possibly saved my life."

She looked closely at him. Dark blue eyes, a strong, square chin, and a nose that appeared to have been broken once or twice. Broad shoulders and a narrow waist, and a gunbelt resting on lean hips. An aura of danger surrounded him, and for a moment she wondered if she'd been saved by someone who was a bigger threat than the one he'd rescued her from.

"Sure looked like he planned to hurt you some, but I don't know that he would've killed you. I'm Landry Mitchell, by the way."

"Olivia Harding." She held out her gloved hand, now covered with dirt and mud. Still, he took it in his, her small hand disappearing in his large work-roughened one. Even through the white satin fabric, his warmth seeped into her, chasing away the chill of what had almost happened.

"Nice to make your acquaintance, ma'am," he said.

He brushed his chestnut-colored hair back off his face with his fingers. It was only then she noticed the gash on the side of his forehead near his temple. Blood trickled down his cheek. "You're hurt!"

"Nothing to worry about. I've been hurt far worse than this." He reached up and wiped the blood from his cheek with the back of his hand.

"You'll need to get Doc Leonard to stitch that up," she said, moving a few steps closer and peering at the jagged wound.

"It's fine."

"Really—"

"Put your hands up, Mitchell." The voice came from behind, startling Olivia. She spun around to see the sheriff, Zane Morgan, and his deputy, Emmett Farris, a few yards away.

Emmett had his gun out of his holster and pointed at Landry's chest. A small crowd had begun to gather behind them, filling the air with voices.

Landry raised his arms in surrender. "Take it easy, Emmett. No need to get yourself all worked up."

"No!" Olivia cried out, moving to stand in front of Landry, shielding him. Surely the deputy wouldn't shoot a woman. "He didn't do anything."

"You all right, Olivia?" Zane asked, his gaze taking in the streaks of dirt on her face and the tear in the sleeve of her green blouse.

"I'm fine," she replied. "Thanks to Mr. Mitchell."

Zane's brows arched. "Is that so?"

"He saved me from ... well, I'd rather not think about what might have happened if he hadn't been here."

As Olivia looked on, Emmett took a few steps toward Landry, his mouth twisting in a sneer. "Getting yourself in trouble again, Mitchell?"

Landry met his gaze squarely. "You'd like that, wouldn't you?"

"You bet I would." Emmett's hatred of Landry was clear in the tone of his voice. "I'd like to see you back behind bars where you belong."

Back behind bars? He was a criminal? He'd saved her from what would likely have been an unspeakable horror, and he'd been nothing but a gentleman. She found it hard to believe he'd been in prison.

Landry's lips quirked. "Sorry to disappoint you, Emmett, but like the lady said, I was just trying to help."

"Emmett." Zane interrupted the confrontation between the two men. "Looks like everything's fine here. Why don't you head on back to the office?"

Emmett's eyes narrowed, but he didn't move. Then, a few tense seconds later, he lowered his Colt and slid it back into the holster. With a final glare in Landry's direction, he turned and stormed off.

Zane watched Emmett go, then turned his attention to the onlookers who'd appeared out of nowhere and were now milling around trying to get a good look. "There's nothing to see here, folks," he said. "Go on home."

He waited until the crowd had dispersed before turning his attention back to Olivia. "Want to tell me what happened?"

As much as she'd rather forget the whole incident, she wanted the man who'd attacked her found and arrested. In as much detail as she could recall, she described everything that had happened up to the time Zane and Emmett arrived.

"He doesn't sound familiar from the description, but since you say he'd been drinking, I'll take a walk over to the saloon and see if there's anyone there that looks like the man you described. Meanwhile, I suggest you pay extra attention for the next little while. What were you doing in this end of town?"

"I was at the orphanage," she said.

"Well, I'd advise you not to go walking around by yourself for a few days, just in case ..." His voice trailed off.

Olivia's eyes widened, and her heartbeat sped up. "You think he might—?"

"Probably not," he said, his voice taking on a tone meant to calm a hysterical child. "He's likely a drifter who'd had too much to drink and you just happened to be in the wrong place at the wrong time. He's probably sleeping it off somewhere or already long gone. But it doesn't hurt to be careful."

"I will."

"And if you see him again, make sure you

stay away from him. Come and get me and let me take care of it."

She nodded.

Zane turned to Landry. "You've got quite a gash there, Mitchell," he said "You might want to get Doc to look at it."

"No thanks. If it's all the same to you, I'll just finish up what I was doing and go back to the livery. I still have work to do before I run out of daylight."

Zane nodded. "Sounds like a good idea. I'll see Olivia home."

"I can't thank you enough," Olivia said, looking up at Landry. "If there's anything I can to do repay you ..."

Landry turned to Olivia. "Glad to be of assistance, ma'am." He went back into the alley to pick up his hat from where it had landed during the scuffle. Brushing off the dirt and dust, he put it on and turned away.

Olivia watched him until he disappeared from view, wishing she could have spent more time with him, getting to know him. Something about him drew her in, a need, a sadness in his eyes that she understood only too well.

But he was a criminal, for heaven's sake.

But if he was free, that meant he'd paid his debt to society, she contradicted herself. Shouldn't he be given a second chance?

Cupping her elbow, Zane guided her down the boardwalk toward the house she'd inherited from a grandfather she'd never met. She'd come to Rocky Ridge to sell the house, but instead, she'd fallen in love with the town and the people who lived there, and had never left.

"You're lucky he was close by." Zane's voice

interrupted her thoughts as if he'd read her mind. "But he's not the kind of man you want to befriend. He and his brother got themselves in a heap of trouble and even though he's kept to himself since he got back, there's no way to know what he might do once his brother gets out."

He might be trouble, Olivia thought, but he had risked his life to save her. He'd ended up with a wound on his forehead, and it could have been so much worse. Her attacker had had a gun, and he could very easily have killed Landry for trying to help her.

"Was he really in prison like Emmett said?"

Zane nodded, but didn't offer any further information.

"What for?" she asked.

"Landry, his brother and another man were convicted of robbing the bank."

"I see." Olivia slowed her steps to a stop.

Zane walked ahead, then realizing she wasn't keeping up with him, turned back to face her. "What's wrong?" he asked.

"Did Mr. Mitchell serve his full sentence?"

"He did."

"Yet your deputy is still treating him like a criminal," she pointed out.

"Folks sometimes find it hard to forgive—"

"Do you believe he deserves a second chance?"

"Look, Olivia," he said, tucking his thumbs into the waist of his pants. "As far as I'm concerned, he served his time and he hasn't gotten himself into any more trouble. As long as it stays that way, we'll get along just fine."

"I'd like to do something for him."

"That's not a good idea," he said. "It would be best if you steer clear of him. He doesn't seem like he'd take too kindly to anybody trying to socialize with him."

She nodded, but something deep in her soul couldn't agree. Something about him touched her, as if ... as if he needed her.

And one thing Olivia couldn't resist was someone in need.

Landry sat alone at a table in the corner of The Lucky Shamrock, his back to the wall. That was one of the first lessons he'd learned in prison. Whenever possible, don't give anyone a chance to attack from behind.

Voices, laughter, and the tinkle of piano keys filled the smoke-laden air. Four cowboys from the Triple M relaxed at the bar, while Doc Leonard and two of the town merchants shared a bottle of whiskey at a table near the back.

Ansel Gerber, the bartender, swiped a glass with a towel and set it on a shelf behind him. He gave Landry a questioning glance, dipping his head to ask silently if he wanted a refill of the beer he'd drained a few seconds before.

Landry shook his head. He knew he should go home, if a bed and a dresser in a room at the back of the livery could be called home. But it was all he had, and even though he'd been out of prison for almost two years, the memory of being caged up like an animal hadn't left him. After living in a cell, a room with a door he could open was still a luxury he'd never again take for granted.

A soft voice interrupted his thoughts.

"Evenin', Landry."

He looked up to see Lulu smiling at him. "Evenin', Lulu."

"Mind if I sit with you a spell?" she asked, her head gesturing to the empty chair beside him. "You're looking lonely."

He shrugged. Lonely? He supposed he was, but what did he expect, coming back to Rocky Ridge? He should have stayed away, like Tobias told him.

People didn't forget, Tobias had said. They didn't forgive. And they sure weren't going to welcome him back with open arms. So why not go somewhere new, somewhere nobody knew him or what had happened to land him behind bars?

But he hadn't listened. The question was, why not? Because he was a glutton for punishment? Or because somewhere deep down he believed people were basically good? That eventually his friends and the people he'd grown up with would accept him again and he could have his life back?

"You're awfully serious tonight, Landry," Lulu said, sliding into the chair beside him, adjusting the skirt of her deep purple satin dress to give him a clear view of her long, shapely legs. "Want to talk about what's eating at you?"

"Nothing." That was a bald-faced lie, but he wasn't about to share his problems with a saloon whore, even if she was the prettiest and nicest of the ladies there.

He was lonely, but that wasn't what was weighing on his mind. His thoughts were filled with a particular woman, a woman with pale yellow curls and brownish-gold eyes surrounded by long, dark lashes. And a smile that seemed to chase away the chill that had filled him since the day six years ago that had changed his life forever.

And even though she'd just had probably the worst experience of her life, she'd been nice to him. But she hadn't known he was an ex-convict then. And even though she'd tried to hide it, he'd seen the surprise and even a little suspicion in her eyes when Emmett had shown up and she'd found out the truth about him.

Before that, he'd sensed something between them, some kind of connection he couldn't explain. And if things were different, he might have thought about pursuing that connection to see where it led.

But he was an outcast who'd likely made a big mistake trying to put the past behind him. She deserved someone better than him, a man she could be proud to be seen with, a man who hadn't spent more than three years in prison.

Lulu reached over and rested her hand on his arm, giving him a smile that was a clear invitation. Her fingers stroked his skin, a motion between a caress and a massage. "I'm sure I could take your mind off whatever's bothering you."

He should let Lulu work her magic. Should take her upstairs and let her make him forget about Olivia Harding. But her touch did nothing for him tonight. In fact, it was downright irritating.

He got up, his chair scraping across the wooden floor. He picked up his hat and put it on.

Lulu stood, waiting, her smile wider. She

made a move to tuck her hand beneath his elbow.

He shrugged it off. "Sorry, Lulu. Not tonight."

The kitchen of the orphanage was bustling with activity the next morning as it usually was when meals were being prepared for the children.

Mirabelle Granger and Ruth Bower sat at the long oak table at one end of the room, their heads bowed and their voices low as they chopped carrots and onions for the soup pot already bubbling on the cast-iron stove in the corner. Liza, a pretty dark-haired girl who had grown up in the orphanage but was now married and expecting her first child, was peeling potatoes at the worktable near the sink.

It occurred to Olivia that she'd been about the same age as Liza when she'd received the inheritance that had brought her to Rocky Ridge.

Voices drifted in the air from the parlor, a large room surrounded by windows where some of the younger children were playing dominoes under the not-so-watchful eye of one of the older boys reading a dog-eared copy of *Moby Dick*.

Olivia scooped up a handful of flour and sprinkled it on the wooden work table, then set the mound of bread dough on top. Tearing the dough into pieces, she began to shape it into rolls.

Almira Potts, the orphanage's matron, waddled across the room and wrapped an arm around Olivia, her breathing labored from the exertion. "You should have stayed home today after what happened ..." Her voice trailed off, as if she couldn't bear to mention the details.

Olivia reached out and patted Almira's hand. "Thank you, Almira, but I'm fine," she lied. "Really."

She was far from fine. Her eyes felt gritty from lack of sleep, every muscle in her body ached from the attack the day before, and she couldn't dismiss the twinge of fear in the back of her mind at the thought of walking home alone later that afternoon.

But she refused to let what had happened keep her away from her work. The children needed her. Almira needed her.

The orphanage was a three-story building at the edge of town that had once been owned by a miner who'd struck it rich several years before. He'd died before he could bring his wife and children to Colorado, and the building had been left to decay.

Almira and her husband had bought it when they'd first arrived in Rocky Ridge, planning to fill it with a large family. Unfortunately, they'd never been blessed with children of their own. Over the years, so Olivia had heard, they'd taken in children who had been orphaned or deserted. When Almira's husband died, she'd somehow managed to find funds to keep the doors open as an orphanage.

Now, the paint was peeling and the front porch sagged, but the inside was filled with love and laughter, all thanks to Almira and her unflagging generosity and energy.

Almira lived in one room on the top floor the building and took a small stipend, her only assistance caring for the children coming from volunteers like Olivia, and the only money coming from donations.

Olivia hadn't even considered staying away that afternoon. That would only add more work to the other women's already heavy load, and leave her with too much time to fret about what had happened – and what might have happened if it hadn't been for Landry Mitchell.

Warmth seeped through her as his image floated into her mind.

"It really was lucky Mr. Mitchell happened by," Almira went on.

Olivia nodded. "It was."

Almira's voice lowered to a whisper. "You do know about him, don't you?"

"Yes, I did hear about his history—"

"I do believe he's paid his debt to society, but at the same time, one never knows if he's truly reformed."

"I'm not sure anyone knows but him."

A twinkle appeared in Almira's eyes, the creases on her wrinkled face deepening. "He is very handsome, though, isn't he?"

Olivia felt her cheeks flush. Almira had echoed her thoughts exactly.

"But he's not the type of man a decent woman should be seen with," Almira went on. "I'm surprised he came back here. He must have known how people around here would react."

"Perhaps he wants to make amends," Olivia suggested.

"Perhaps." Almira set the formed dough onto a baking sheet. "But sometimes, it's not possible for a man to just pick up where he left off and expect others to forget the past."

Almira moved away, taking the baking sheet with

her to another table while Olivia continued filling
another tray with rolls.

While she worked, she couldn't put Landry out of
her mind. There were hundreds of small towns
popping up all over the west. It would have been so
much easier for him to settle somewhere else,
somewhere where no one knew about him and his
past, and no one would judge him.

So why *had* he come back?

Chapter Two

Landry swung the hammer, the clang of metal against metal filling the silence as he molded the horseshoe into shape. Sweat dripped down his face and onto the anvil.

Setting the hammer aside, he grabbed a pair of tongs and picked up the horseshoe to study the form and shape, making sure it was as perfect as possible. A shoe didn't do much good if it didn't fit the horse's hoof. Then he dipped the horseshoe into the tub of cold water nearby, keeping it at arm's length until the steam cleared and the water stopped sizzling and spitting bubbles into the air.

He'd learned the hard way not to stand too close. He had the healed burns on his forearms to show for his ignorance.

Of course, those burns came from working alongside Rufus Macklin back in Silverdale when he first got out of prison.

A faint smile tugged at his lips at the memory. One of the few men who'd been willing to take a chance on him, Rufus had taught Landry everything he knew about blacksmithing.

And when Rufus passed on and Landry

found himself unemployed, luck had been on his side. He'd heard the livery stable in Rocky Ridge was for sale, and he'd made the decision to come home.

He hadn't expected to be welcomed with open arms, but he sure hadn't thought he'd be treated like a pariah. And if there'd been another blacksmith in town, he was pretty sure he'd never get any business from most of the folks in town at all. Even his old friends had turned their backs on him.

But that was fine with him. He didn't need them. He didn't need anybody. As long as he had enough money to feed himself, he didn't need more.

Satisfied that the horseshoe was as perfect as he could make it, he set it aside, wiped his hands with a cloth and headed to the water bucket for a drink. He was lifting the ladle to his lips when a female voice called his name.

"Mr. Mitchell?"

Startled, the ladle slipped. Water splashed over the sides of the bucket as the bowl of the ladle fell into the water.

He recognized that voice. The soft silky sound had filled his thoughts and fantasies his entire sleepless night before.

He'd never expected to see Olivia Harding again. Why would he? They didn't exactly run in the same social circles, and the only people who even spoke to him these days were the men who spent their evenings in the saloon and the few customers who needed their horses shod or their farm equipment repaired. So what was she doing here?

He turned, squinting into the shaft of

sunlight streaming through the open doors. Silhouetted against the light, she moved toward him, her slim hips swaying, her skirt brushing against the dirt floor. A sudden surge of lust blazed through him, settling low in his belly.

He swore inwardly. He'd been without a woman for far too long.

Coming out of the shadows, she stopped in front of him, close enough that he could see the sweet smile on her face, her eyes sparkling. Her lavender scent washed over him.

"Good afternoon, Mr. Mitchell," she said.

"You shouldn't be in here." As soon as the words left his mouth, he regretted them. His voice had been sharper than he'd intended, and her smile quickly faded. "I mean, it's dirty in here. No place for a woman," he added, doing his best to lighten the tone of his voice. He didn't want her here, but at the same time, he hadn't meant to hurt her feelings.

The smile returned. "Oh, heavens, that doesn't matter. I've been in dirtier places than this, and I didn't expect a livery stable to be spick and span."

"What can I do for you?"

"I ... I wanted to see ... to check on you ..."

"I'm fine."

"Your head—?"

"Stopped bleeding," he interrupted, his lips quirking in a smile.

"I'm so sorry about the way Emmett treated you yesterday."

"Don't worry about it. I'm used to it." Emmett's words were nothing compared to some that had been hurled at him over the past few years.

"Oh ..."

"Is there something else?"

Her head lowered and she studied her hands for a few seconds before finally looking up at him, as if she was trying to find a reason to stay. But why would she? He was pretty sure Zane Morgan had filled her in, had told her in detail who he was and why he'd been in prison.

"The sheriff told me about you," she said, "but I prefer to judge people for myself, not because of some idle gossip—"

He wasn't surprised that she'd been warned to stay away from him. But he didn't care. At least that's what he'd been telling himself. "Even when the gossip is true?"

"Even then."

He turned his back on her and moved away, making a pretense of being busy cleaning up. He didn't need her sympathy. "So you know it's not going to help your reputation if somebody sees you here."

"Mr. Mitchell." She followed him, moving around him until they were face to face. "I know how difficult it is to start over, but I'd like to help."

The softness in her voice seeped through him, filling him like a cup of cocoa on a winter's day. Kindness he didn't dare let himself accept. He let out a laugh, failing to keep the tinge of bitterness out of his voice.   "Look, Miss Harding—"

"Olivia."

"Okay, Olivia. I don't mean to hurt your feelings, but I'll say it plain and simple. I don't need your help."

"I'm only trying to—"

He locked gazes with her. "I'll say it again," he said. "I don't need your help. I don't want your help. I'm fine with the way things are. So why don't you move along and go find somebody else to fix?"

She took a step back, almost as if he'd physically assaulted her. He'd been mean, cruel. But the woman wouldn't take no for an answer, so there was no other way to get rid of her except by being blunt.

"Would you like you to come to supper tonight?" she went on as if she hadn't heard a word he'd said. "I feel responsible for your injury and although I can never repay you for your bravery, I can offer you a home-cooked meal." She glanced around, her gaze stopping on the open door to the room where he slept. "It seems to me you could use one."

Picking up the hammer he'd set aside earlier, he looked down at her. "I appreciate the offer, but I don't think that's a good idea."

"But—"

"Look," he began, "I don't need a home-cooked meal. I don't need your sympathy. And I sure don't need you coming around here like some do-gooder looking for somebody to save. Now if there's nothing else, old Sundown over there needs a new shoe so I need to get back to work."

She nodded, gazing up at him with disappointment filling her huge golden-brown eyes.

"Of course," she said. "I understand. I apologize for taking up your time. Good day."

As he watched her walk away, he slammed the hammer back down on the table beside him. He'd hurt her. He knew that. Even as the cruel words had spilled from his mouth, he'd hated himself for saying them. But if he hadn't been so direct, he had a feeling she'd keep coming back time and again until she wore him down.

And that was the last thing he needed. She was prettier than a flower, and her sweet perfume and the way she moved managed to make him want to get to know her, to spend time with her, to find out if the strange feelings he'd noticed whenever she was near were because of her or something else.

And if they were because of her ... well, those were feelings he couldn't allow himself to act on, just in case he became attracted to her even more than he already was.

She was the kind of woman who made him wish there was a possibility of a future ... a future with a respectable woman ... a family ...

But he'd learned one thing since he'd gotten out of prison - there was no point wishing for things he couldn't have.

Olivia could barely hear herself think over the ruckus in the orphanage dining room. Unlike many of the other institutions of its kind, Almira encouraged the children to laugh, to talk, to enjoy their lives as much as possible. She loved every one of the children she cared for, and treated each of them like her own.

Olivia sat at one end of the table, her heart full, her gaze taking in the chatter and laughter as the children ate their meals. For one reason or another, every one of the children here no longer had families who could take care of them. Two of the boys had been found in an alley, digging through scraps for food. Almira had rescued one of the older girls in the nick of time from a saloon in the next town. Some had been brought by relatives after the children's parents had died, while others, like the baby she was feeding, had been left on the doorstep.

Every one of the children needed love and care, and Olivia couldn't think of anything else she'd rather do.

The only thing Olivia had ever wanted was a family of her own. Now, at twenty-three, she was an old maid, a spinster. The likelihood of her ever marrying and having her own children grew more and more remote every day. It saddened her that the only children she'd ever be able to love were someone else's.

Her glance stilled when it reached Daniel, the newest addition to the growing number of children living at the orphanage. He was sitting quietly beside her, his meal untouched. He hadn't spoken or eaten more than a mouthful of food since he'd been left there three days before. All she or Almira had been able to find out from the uncle who'd left him there was that he was seven years old, he'd lived on a farm, and his parents had been killed in an accident a few weeks before.

Olivia's heart went out to him. She couldn't imagine being alone at such a young age, although all the children who lived there were in the same situation.

Still, something about Daniel had found a soft spot inside her and he'd stolen a piece of her heart.

"Don't you like stew?" she asked.

For a moment, he didn't answer. Then he raised his head and looked at her. His eyes were huge in his small face. He shook his head.

"You must be hungry. You didn't eat breakfast either."

He shrugged, slumped further down into the chair and hung his head.

The baby in Olivia's arms squirmed, letting the milk from the bottle dribble down his chin. Olivia quickly wiped the milk away, then picked him up and rested him on her shoulder, gently rubbing his back until she heard him burp.

A few seconds later, Olivia arched her neck so she could steal a peek at the infant. He was fast asleep. "I'll take the baby upstairs," she whispered to Almira. "I'll be back in a few minutes."

By the time she came back downstairs, the room was empty except for two of the older girls clearing the table. Daniel's plate hadn't been touched.

Worry tugged at Olivia. They'd left him, assuming that when he was hungry enough, he would eat. How long could a child go without food? she wondered. Surely not much longer.

"It seems Daniel doesn't like stew," she told Almira as she stacked the dirty plates on the work table to be washed.

Almira set the pot of leftover stew in the icebox and closed the door. "I'd like to offer each of the children what they like, but it would be impossible to satisfy every one of them. We'd never be finished cooking."

"I know, but I'm worried. He's going to get sick if he doesn't eat soon,'" Olivia said.

Almira nodded. "I don't know what else we can do."

"I don't either."

Olivia was still pondering the problem on her way home later that afternoon. Surely there must be something that would tempt him to eat.

Chocolate. She'd never met a child who didn't like chocolate. She chuckled to herself. Now that she thought of it, she'd never met a grown-up who didn't like chocolate either.

Turning back, she hurried along the boardwalk to the mercantile. Elias Todd looked up from counting nails when the bell above the door jingled and she went inside. "Afternoon, Miss Olivia," he called out with a wave. "What can I get you today?"

She smiled and returned his greeting. "Do you have any chocolate?"

The shopkeeper dropped the handful of nails he was holding into a bag, then wiped his hands on a cloth. "You're in luck. Got a new supply in just this morning."

"That's wonderful." Olivia mentally sifted through the recipes she had on hand at home, mentally calculating what other ingredients she'd need.

Eager to start baking a batch of cookies she hoped Daniel wouldn't be able to resist, she hurried home with her purchases. On the way, she'd also made a decision. She'd make enough cookies for the children at the orphanage, but she'd set some aside to take to Landry, too. She suspected that, living alone, he rarely got any kind of desserts or sweets, and everyone needed a treat now and then.

She shouldn't worry about him. He'd made it quite clear he didn't want her to bother him. Yet something about him – perhaps the loneliness she saw in his eyes in spite of the way he pushed people away – drew her to him.

That he was lonely was obvious to her. She recognized it because she suffered from the same affliction. Although she made a point of being surrounded by people as much as possible, when she closed her door in the evening, she was alone. No husband, no children, no one who loved her. No family of her own.

It seemed Landry was even worse off than she was. He didn't even have a home, just a room in a livery stable, and from what she'd heard from Zane and the ladies at the orphanage that morning, his only family was still in prison. The difference was that he'd convinced himself that he didn't need anyone. That he was content to be alone.

But he was wrong.

Everyone needed someone, even if it was just a friend. And for Landry, she decided, that someone would be her.

Chapter Three

The little girl's sudden howl drowned out the other children's voices in the parlor of the orphanage.

Olivia dropped the carrot she was peeling and ran, wiping her hands on her apron as she raced through the house toward the room that had grown suspiciously quiet.

Several pairs of eyes watched as she entered the parlor. Scanning the room, her glance landed on four-year-old Sadie Morrison lying on the carpet. Sadie's face was pale, but her cries had lessened to quiet sobs.

The children moved away as Olivia hurried to the little girl's side. "What happened?" she asked, looking first at Sadie then scanning each of the children's faces. No one answered.

Olivia asked again, her voice a little louder this time.

Sadie looked up at Olivia. Her eyes were bright with tears that clung to her eyelashes. "I fell," she murmured.

"How?"

Several of the boys hung their heads. Others

looked away. Finally, Jeremiah Porter spoke up. "We wath playing," he began through two missing front teeth. "And Thadie thlipped."

"Can you move your leg?" Olivia asked Sadie, crouching down and gathering her in a gentle hug.

Sadie sniffled. "My ankle hurts."

Already it had started to swell, and Olivia feared it might be broken. Only a doctor would be able to tell. Scooping Sadie into her arms, Olivia got up and headed toward the door. "Jeremiah, Mrs. Potts is in the washhouse. Go and tell her I've taken Sadie to the doctor and I'll be back as soon as I can."

The other children in the room stood quietly while Jeremiah rushed off.

"I want the rest of you to clean up this room, then each of you take a book and read silently until Mrs. Potts comes inside. Do you understand?"

They nodded in unison.

With Sadie in her arms, Olivia hurried out of the house and along the boardwalk toward Doc Leonard's clinic.

It didn't take long before Olivia was exhausted from carrying Sadie. Her arms ached, and her back and legs strained under the girl's weight. She should have sent one of the older children to fetch the doctor, but the thought hadn't even crossed her mind. All she'd thought about was getting help for Sadie.

A voice calling her name from behind startled her, probably more because of her recent experience than the voice itself. She spun around in time to see Landry striding toward her, his brow creased in a frown.

He held out his arms. "Here, let me carry her for you."

"Oh ... no ... it's fine ..."

Landry smiled gently at Sadie, and Olivia's heart tripped. She hadn't thought it possible that a smile could make him even more handsome.

"Would it be all right if I carry you for a little while?" Landry asked Sadie. His deep voice held a tenderness Olivia didn't expect. "Miss Olivia's arms are tired."

For a few seconds, it seemed Sadie would refuse. Her small face pursed in a frown as she studied him, but then she nodded and held her arms out for Landry to lift her out of Olivia's arms.

The sudden weightlessness made Olivia's arms tingle, and she shook them out at her sides until the blood flowed through them again. "Thank you, but it really wasn't necessary," she said. "I could have managed—"

"I know you could have, but it's easier for me. Where are you going?"

"I hurted my leg," Sadie put in, gazing up at Landry.

"We're going to the clinic," Olivia replied.

Sadie's eyes never left Landry's face. "See?" She straightened her leg to show Landry her swollen ankle. "Do you think it's broke?"

Landry pretended to study the ankle. "I only take care of horses, not people, so I think we'd best let the doctor figure that out."

Said nodded, then wiggled until she was settled comfortably in Landry's arms.

Olivia was surprised at how quickly Sadie

had taken to Landry as if she'd known him all her life. Yet another good quality, she mused.

"Well then," Landry said, interrupting Olivia's stray thoughts, "we'd better get a move on instead of standing here talking."

Without another word, he strode off, his heavy footsteps thudding on the boardwalk. Olivia had to hurry to catch up, and neither of them spoke again until they reached the clinic. Both Grace Leonard and her father were physicians, and today, Grace greeted them when Olivia opened the door and held it open for Landry to carry Sadie inside.

Olivia was surprised to see Grace in the clinic, since she was very close to delivering her first child. "Shouldn't you be resting?" she asked, keeping an eye on Landry as he gently lowered Sadie to a padded table in the center of the examination room.

Grace massaged her lower back as she waddled across to the table. "Other than not being able to sleep comfortably, I feel fine," she answered with a smile. "It won't be long now, though. The baby is very low now ..."

Landry stepped away from the table and hovered beside the door. "If it's all right with you, I'll just wait outside."

Olivia did her best to hide the smile threatening to erupt. It seemed he was uncomfortable with their talk of babies and childbirth. "You don't have to wait," she told him. "I can manage."

"I don't mind carrying her back when you're ready."

As if he couldn't wait a moment longer, he pulled the door open and hurried out. The chuckle Olivia had been trying to hide escaped, and both she and Grace shared a knowing glance.

Olivia moved to stand beside Sadie, wrapping one arm around her small shoulder. Sadie squeezed Olivia's hand as Grace gently examined the little girl's ankle. Twice, Sadie cried out in pain, but soon, Grace straightened and smiled. "It's not broken, but it is sprained. I'll bandage it up and give her something for pain. It'll likely make her sleepy so I'd like you to stay a few minutes until I'm sure she doesn't have any adverse effects."

While the laudanum took effect, Grace rested on a hardback chair in the corner of the room. "Until now, I had no idea what expectant mothers went through," she said with a wry smile. "Now that I have first-hand experience, I'll understand better."

"I doubt I'll ever have that experience," Olivia said, unable to prevent the tinge of sadness in her voice. She'd wanted a family of her own as far back as she could remember.

"You will," Grace assured her. "I'm sure there are at least a dozen men in town who'd be happy to court you if you'd give them a chance."

"None that I'd be inclined to marry."

Grace struggled to her feet and crossed to where Sadie was lying on the padded table. Her eyes were drifting closed. "You'd be surprised where you might find love. I certainly was."

"Then I'll keep an open mind."

"I hope so. Now, it looks like Sadie hasn't had a reaction to the medicine. I think it's safe to take her home now."

As he'd promised, Landry was sitting on a bench outside, his back leaning against the wall with his eyes closed when Olivia opened the door.

Her breath caught in her throat. In sleep, with his features relaxed, he was even more handsome. She called his name softly, and moments later, he was hurrying inside.

"Please let me know if there's anything I can do to help, either before or after the baby comes," Olivia said as they were leaving.

Grace smiled. "I will."

Silently, Landry and Olivia made their way back along the boardwalk. Landry had scooped Sadie up as if she weighed no more than a feather, and now, her head rested on his shoulder, her eyes closed. She would likely stay asleep until they reached the orphanage.

"I appreciate your help," Olivia said. "It seems you're always coming to my rescue."

"It's no problem. Just happened to see you struggling with her."

"Working for Mr. Raye again?"

Landry nodded. "Not much business at the livery since I got back."

She glanced up at him, taking note of the way his eyes had darkened and a muscle in his jaw had tightened as he spoke.

"Why did you come back here?" she asked before she could stop herself. Her cheeks heated at the impropriety of her question. His motives were none of her business.

"That's a good question."

Olivia thought she heard a note of despair in his voice, but then he shifted Sadie in his arms and lengthened his steps, striding ahead.

She shouldn't care about Landry Mitchell.

But Heaven help her, she did. Something about him appealed to her the way no other man had, made her want to know him better. Made her want to see him smile again.

Both Zane and Almira had warned her against having any future contact with him. They could be right. She could regret getting more involved with him.

But then, Olivia had always had to learn her lessons for herself.

Landry leaned against one of the posts outside the orphanage, the porch roof shading him from the noonday sun. He folded his arms across his chest and crossed his ankles as he watched a squirrel scurry up the trunk of an oak tree and disappear inside.

What was wrong with him? He should walk away now, go back to the undertaker's and finish polishing the marble tombstone Martin had carved instead of waiting for Olivia.

She'd mentioned on the way back to the orphanage that she'd be going home as soon as she got Sadie settled. He'd told himself he was only waiting to make sure she got home safely and that the man who'd attacked her was nowhere close, but if he was being honest with himself, that was only partially true.

He knew he shouldn't, knew he should stay away from her, but he wanted to talk to her again. Hell, the only women he'd even talked to since he got out of prison were whores, and not one of them could carry on a real conversation.

Sadie had fallen asleep soon after they'd left

the clinic, and he'd found himself enjoying the short time he'd had with Olivia as they'd walked back to the orphanage.

It sure wouldn't help her reputation to be seen with him, but she didn't seem to mind, and he doubted he could damage it too much by seeing her safely home after what had happened.

But after today, he'd stay away from her, he promised himself.

The door opened and Olivia stepped outside. She smiled when she saw him waiting. "What are you still doing here?" she asked.

He straightened and crossed the porch to where she was standing near the stairs. "Thought I'd make sure you got home safe."

"Oh ... that's not necessary ... but thank you ..."

As they strolled down the boardwalk toward her house on the other side of town, Landry was aware of the curious glances being sent their way as well as those who turned their heads and ignored them.

Olivia, on the other hand, was oblivious, chattering away about the weather, the children, the barn dance the next week. "It does seem strange to me that they call it a barn dance when it's held outside, but no matter what it's called, I'm looking forward to it. Are you going?" she asked.

"Not planning to."

"Why not?"

He shrugged.

"Have you ever attended?"

"No."

"I hear it's held every year, but last year was the first time for me," Olivia said.

Landry nodded. "It's been going on as far back as I can remember. Nobody seems to know how or why it started, but it's tradition now. Every year, more and more people come from all over."

"Except you."

"Except me."

"Why didn't you ever attend?"

He didn't really have a good answer, except that by the time he was old enough to enjoy it, he was busy with the farm. "Never found time."

"Perhaps this time you could find a few minutes?"

The question hung in the air. "I'm not much of a dancer," he said, his lips quirking in a wry grin.

"It's never too late to learn," she pointed out.

"I suppose that's true."

For the next few minutes, they strolled along the boardwalk, both lost in their own thoughts.

"Are you happy to be back?" Olivia asked as they passed Brett Morgan's law office and stepped off the boardwalk to go around a corner to a cluster of houses on a makeshift street.

"Hasn't worked out the way I thought it would," he replied. Coming back to Rocky Ridge had been everything he'd dreamed of while he was behind bars, but his return hadn't lived up to the fantasy.

Folks crossed the street to avoid him. The only business he got was because there wasn't anybody else who could fix the axles on their wagons, shoe their horses or repair their plows, and even most of his friends from before wanted nothing to do with him now.

There were a few who seemed willing to let the past die, though. The sheriff, for one, and Trey and Claire Morgan, the owners of The Lucky Shamrock. Not to mention some of the hands from the Triple M Ranch, the spread a few miles from town. But there weren't enough people who were willing to give him a second chance to make him feel at home again.

"Perhaps it would have been easier to go somewhere else, to start fresh ..." Olivia said softly.

"The easiest way to do something isn't always the best way or the right way," he said. "I grew up here, and I wanted that life back, thought I could get that life back. But it's not that simple. Folks here don't forgive easily. And they sure don't forget."

"Then you have to show the town that they're wrong, that you should be forgiven, that you can be trusted again."

He let out a short laugh. "And how am I supposed to do that?"

"Come to church on Sunday," she said. "That would be a start. Perhaps if they see you're asking forgiveness from God, they'll be more likely to forgive you, too."

"Me and God don't get along ..."

Olivia stopped in front of a small house with a gabled roof, long windows and a porch that ran the length of the house. Bright pink flowers lined a pathway to a set of wide steps leading up to the porch. Two rocking chairs sat side-by-side near the door. "This is home," she said.

"It's nice."

"Thank you for walking me home. Can I offer

you some tea?"

He wanted to stay, wanted more than anything to relax in one of the rocking chairs on the porch and enjoy a glass of tea with Olivia, but he sure didn't want to get used to having her to talk to. In fact, he was surprised she'd been willing to let him walk her home.

"Thanks, but I have work to do at the livery," he lied.

An awkward silence fell over them. Somewhere nearby a cat meowed, followed by a child's voice trying to coax the cat to come closer.

"Then perhaps I'll see you on Sunday?"

Hell, he hadn't been in church in years, and while he was in prison, he was pretty sure God had forgotten all about him. "I don't know ..."

Olivia rested her hand on his forearm, the warmth of her touch flowing through him. "Please, just think about it. If you want your life back, you have to be willing to make an effort to get it."

Her golden-brown eyes searched his face. Was she right? Or was she giving people more credit than they deserved? Tipping his hat, he gave her a faint smile. "I'll think about it."

On Sunday morning, Olivia took one last look in the mirror, tucking a stray curl into the knot at the nape of her neck. She pinched her cheeks to give them a little color, then carefully placed her lilac silk and lace bonnet on her hair, tying the ribbons into a perfect bow under her chin.

Smoothing a wrinkle from the lilac and white dress she'd chosen to wear, she picked up her matching reticule and Bible and left the house.

A few dark clouds in the distance marred the otherwise clear blue sky, but she wasn't concerned. She didn't have far to walk if it started to rain.

She was later than usual leaving, so she had to hurry to reach the church before the service began.

As she expected, the small church was almost full by the time Olivia stepped inside and slid into an empty pew near the door.

As she smoothed a few creases in the skirt of her dress, the door opened behind her and a family from a nearby farm came inside. The man led his family to an empty pew on the other side of the aisle. As they were settling in, John Winters, the pastor, took his place behind the pulpit.

"Good morning," he began, "and welcome ..." His voice died out as the door opened once again and Landry walked in. He paused just inside and pulled the door closed behind him, then tugged his hat off his head and raked his fingers through his hair.

"And welcome to you, Mr. Mitchell," he continued. All eyes turned toward him, and hushed mutterings spread through the small congregation.

Olivia saw the muscle in Landry's jaw tense, and for a moment, she wondered if he'd turn around and leave. She was glad he'd listened to her advice and had decided to come, but she wouldn't really blame him if he did leave. This was a huge step for him, and she was sure he'd hoped to slip in unnoticed instead of becoming the center of attention.

But instead of walking out, he met the pastor's gaze squarely and nodded, acknowledging the man's greeting.

The pastor resumed his welcome message, but his words were lost on Olivia. Landry was the focus of her attention, her skin tingling and that same unfamiliar sensation settling inside her when she looked at him. He'd shaved and was dressed in a dark blue jacket and white shirt that emphasized his sun-bronzed face.

As if he sensed her presence, he turned his head and their eyes met. She gave him an encouraging smile, and gestured with a slight bob of her head to the empty space beside her.

He hesitated for a moment before sliding into the pew beside her.

She leaned a little closer, whispering. "I'm glad you came."

He smiled but didn't answer.

Olivia turned her attention back to the pastor at the front of the church. Landry laid his hat on the seat beside him and sat with his back ramrod straight, his eyes focused on something directly ahead.

As if the pastor had somehow known Landry would be in church that particular day, he spoke about sin, about atonement, and about forgiveness. Several times, Olivia cast a sideways glance in Landry's direction to see how the pastor's words were affecting him, but his expression was set in stone. And while Olivia usually enjoyed the pastor's Sunday sermons, she was pleased when this one was over.

As he did every Sunday, the pastor thanked

each one of the congregation for attending as they left the church and filed out onto the grassy area outside. Dark clouds had replaced the blue sky, and a breeze had whipped up, rustling the leaves in the trees and forming small whirlwinds of dust.

Landry had walked off as soon as the service was over, and as she stood with a few friends, her eyes kept searching for him. A faint smile she couldn't prevent tugged at her lips when she caught a glimpse of Grace's father, the older Doc Leonard, shaking his hand. A few moments later, Landry smiled at something the doctor had said.

Goodness, his smile was intoxicating, she couldn't help thinking, even when that smile wasn't directed at her.

"Olivia?" Almira's voice filtered through Olivia's brain.

"Hmm? Oh ... I'm sorry ... what were you saying?"

"Just wondering what it is about that man that has you all aflutter."

Heat surged into Olivia's cheeks. "Why ... nothing ..."

Almira gently patted Olivia's arm. "You're a grown woman, able to make your own decisions, but you know how folks will react if you start spending time with him, so consider the consequences carefully."

"Yes, of course," Olivia replied as Almira squeezed her hand and said goodbye.

Almira's warning sat heavily in Olivia's chest. She was well aware how most of the town felt about Landry, but she couldn't help being drawn to him.

Taking in another stray, her mother would

have scolded. You can't save everybody.

But it was more than that. It wasn't just that he needed a friend. She couldn't define exactly what it was, but even though she'd been warned he was dangerous, he made her feel safe. And wanted. Even when he'd told her to go away, she sensed he didn't mean it, that he had some unspoken reason for dismissing her.

She caught Landry approaching out of the corner of her eye. She smiled up at him when he stopped beside her. "I'm so glad you came today," she said, then chuckled. "I said that before, didn't I?"

"You did," he replied. "But it doesn't look like some folks are too happy about it."

"Some may not be, but I'm sure others will be pleased to see you're trying to make amends for your past mistakes."

"Maybe."

"Be patient."

He glanced up at the sky. "I'd best be going," he said, ignoring her comment. "You should be getting home, too. Looks like a storm's brewing."

He jammed his hat back on his head, touched the brim with his index finger in a farewell gesture and turned away.

Olivia couldn't explain it, but something inside her wouldn't let him leave. She had to try again. "Landry?" she called out.

He stopped long enough for her to step around him and face him. "Would you like to come to supper tonight?"

"Like I told you before, I don't think it's a good idea—"

"Why not? Do you have other plans?"

"Well ... no ..."

"And you do have to eat, don't you?"

"Sure, but—"

"Unless you dislike me," she put in, her voice rising a notch. What if that was it? What if he just plain didn't like her? A heavy weight settled in her stomach at the thought.

"Hell, no ... oh, sorry, my mouth gets away from me sometimes ... it's not that ..."

"Then what is it?"

"I don't need your sympathy or your help—"

"Yes, you made that quite clear, but I'm not inviting you because I'm trying to help you. I ..." She felt the heat surging into her cheeks and she was sure he could see her cheeks reddening. "I want to get to know you better. Nothing more." She was being inappropriately forward. Proper ladies did not speak of their attraction to a man, especially to the man involved.

"Is that so?"

Well, she thought, as her mother used to say, 'In for a penny, in for a pound.' "Yes," she said, her lips quirking in a smile. "I realize this is highly improper, but—"

"Okay."

Olivia had already mentally prepared another argument, so his sudden acceptance rendered her speechless.

A slow grin lifted his lips. "Regretting the invitation already?"

"Oh, no ... not at all."

"Good. I'll come, but on one condition."

"Condition?"

He nodded. "You invite somebody else, too. Having me as a guest in your house won't help your reputation any, especially if we're alone."

"I don't care about—"

He held up a hand to stop her. "I appreciate that, but for your sake, I'm insisting on this. So if you know somebody else who wouldn't mind having supper with an ex-convict, I'll be there."

"That's silly—"

"That's the way it has to be."

For a few moments, Olivia tried to come up with something that would convince Landry he was being overly cautious, but by the closed expression in his eyes, she realized she'd be wasting her time. He'd made up his mind, and it appeared Landry was the type of man who didn't change it once he'd made a decision.

"Fine," she said, "but only because it makes you feel more comfortable. I don't have an issue with you and I being alone. I'll invite Zane and Priscilla then."

His brows arched. "The sheriff?"

"Priscilla, his wife, is my best friend," she said. Then a smile tugged at her lips. "And who's been around more ... men like you ... than Zane?"

"I doubt even the sheriff will be happy about socializing with me, but if you can convince him, that's fine with me."

She would convince him. And if she couldn't, she knew Priscilla would. She grinned. A raindrop hit her nose, but she barely noticed. Inside, she felt as if she was suddenly filled with sunshine.

Chapter Four

Landry cursed. Loudly. What the hell had he been thinking? He had no business having supper or anything else with Olivia Harding.

She was one of those do-gooders who wanted to fix everybody. He'd figured that out almost as soon as they'd met. But he couldn't be fixed. Nothing she could do would erase his past, make folks forget what he'd done.

Maybe he should have gone somewhere else like his brother suggested, somewhere far away where nobody knew him. But Rocky Ridge was home. He'd spent his whole life there, and for some reason he couldn't define, he wanted to live out his days there. He only wished he knew how to get back to the life he'd had before he'd gotten himself into a situation he couldn't escape.

His brother had warned him. Before Landry was released from prison, Tobias had told him he could never go home. But he hadn't listened. Lately he'd been wondering more and more if maybe Tobias was right.

The thought lodged in his brain as he rode to the livery stable and dismounted near the corral. Maybe he should have stayed away from Rocky Ridge.

But it was too late now. He'd spent every cent he'd saved working for Rufus to buy the livery here in town. Even if he could sell it, he wasn't ready to start fresh somewhere else, back working for somebody else.

He liked working for himself, and even though he didn't have much business, he had enough to get by. And that was all he really cared about.

He stood for a few seconds, his arm resting on his horse's neck as he glanced along the main street. People bustled about, wagons rolled by, children played. It was as if he'd never left. Nothing had changed about the town, only the people in it.

And they'd changed because of what he'd done. He had nobody to blame but himself.

The livery was at the edge of town. Behind him, houses had popped up over the past few years as the population grew. Some were grand two-story houses with picket fences and gardens, while others were little more than one or two-room cabins.

He turned and started walking his horse into the livery. Suddenly, movement out of the corner of his eye caught his attention.

Squinting into the sun, he recognized Curtis Mooney by the limp he'd been left with when he'd been almost crushed to death a few years ago when his horse stumbled and threw him.

Not giving it much thought, Landry took a few steps toward the entrance to the livery, his eyes still on Mooney. The man was struggling to drag a ladder across the space between his barn and his house.

Landry stopped. What was Mooney doing? The man had to be at least seventy and frail as a newborn colt. As Landry looked on, Mooney leaned the ladder against the side of the house and set his foot on the first rung.

"Oh, hell," Landry muttered as the old man began to climb the ladder. He was half way up when it wobbled, and for a second or two, Landry forgot to breathe, a vision filling his mind of the ladder toppling over and taking Mooney with it.

He should leave Mooney to deal with whatever happened. The man hadn't so much as said hello to him since he got back home. But Mooney was likely going to break his neck if somebody didn't step in.

Landry's conscience wouldn't let him stand back and watch somebody get hurt when he could do something to prevent it.

And maybe, just maybe, this was one of those opportunities Olivia had been talking about. In an instant, he'd wound his gelding's reins around the hitching post outside the livery and broken into a run, moving as fast as he could over the uneven ground toward Mooney's cabin.

By the time he got there, the old man had reached the top rung of the ladder and had stretched one leg out, trying to span the distance between the ladder and the roof.

Landry grabbed the ladder and tried to hold it steady. He hesitated to call out in case it surprised Mooney and the old man lost his balance. But the chances of him getting on that roof the way he was going were a hundred to one.

"Mr. Mooney." Landry spoke as calmly and softly as he could manage. As he expected,

Mooney turned suddenly, the grip he had on the ladder loosening. Realizing he was about to fall, he flailed about, finally wrapping his fingers around one of the rungs.

"What in tarnation you trying to do?" Mooney's voice was raspy. "Coming up behind a man like that."

Landry apologized. "Got a leak in your roof?"

"You think I'm up here for the good of my health?" A few seconds later, he added, "Fixing some shingles that came off in the last storm."

"Why don't you come down off there and let me fix the roof for you?"

Mooney glared at Landry. "I didn't ask for your help, so go back where you came from and leave me be."

Landry bristled, even though he was used to comments like that by now. "Look, Mr. Mooney, I know you didn't ask. I'm offering."

"Why? What's in it for you?"

Tempted as he was to walk away and let the old man kill himself, he couldn't do it. "Just trying to be neighborly. That's a big job for one man." He almost pointed out that Mooney was too old to be wandering around on a roof, but caught himself just in time. He was pretty sure Mooney wouldn't appreciate being told he wasn't capable of taking care of his own property.

Landry made a point of looking up at the slate-grey sky. "Looks like that's going to take a while to fix and even though it's stopped raining for now, who knows when it'll start again?"

Mooney glanced up at the dark clouds, but said nothing.

Landry picked up a stack of cedar shingles, set a foot on the bottom rung of the ladder and gave Mooney a questioning glance.

Almost imperceptibly, Mooney nodded.

Less than an hour later, the leak was sealed and new shingles were in place.

Mooney cleared his throat once they were back on the ground. The whole time they were on the roof, no words had been exchanged other than what were absolutely necessary. "Uh ... thanks ..." he said grudgingly.

"Glad to help any time," Landry replied. "If you need something else done, you come get me. Will you do that?"

Mooney didn't answer, but he hadn't refused. Landry walked away, a hint of a smile tugging at his lips. It was a start.

Olivia bustled around the kitchen, humming a tune while she trimmed the pastry from the apple pie she planned to bake for dessert. The aroma of roasting beef and vegetables filled the air

The rain had stopped, and now sunlight streamed through the window, brightening her already joyful mood.

She grinned as she cut two slits in the top of the pastry to allow steam to escape then set the plate aside.

She'd just taken off her apron and hung it on a hook when she heard the knock at the door. Her heartbeat stuttered. Even though he'd said he'd come, she hadn't really expected him to. At most, she'd expected him to send a message saying something had come up.

But he hadn't. He was here!

Crossing to the door, she smoothed down the skirt of her dress, then tucked a stray curl back into the ribbon holding her hair at the nape of her neck.

Landry was standing on the porch with his back to her when she opened the door. "Afternoon, Landry," she said softly.

He spun around to face her and returned her greeting.

She opened the door wider to admit him. "You came."

"I'll admit I wasn't going to."

"What changed your mind?"

He shrugged. "I don't really know."

"Well, then," she said brightly, "you're here now, and I'm sure Zane and Priscilla will be along shortly. Come inside and let me get you a glass of lemonade while supper is cooking."

"If it's all the same to you, can we sit on the porch until they get here? I like to be outside as much as I can, and I miss having a porch."

Olivia hadn't thought of what Landry had lost when he went to prison. Friends, yes. But more than that, simple pleasures she took for granted. "Of course," she said. "Why don't you make yourself comfortable and I'll bring us some lemonade?"

"That would be nice."

While Landry waited on the porch, Olivia hurried inside and put the pie in the oven. Then she poured two glasses of lemonade, put them on a tray and went back outside. Landry was slowly rocking in one of the chairs, so she sat down in the chair beside him and set the tray on a table between them. "Here you are," she said, handing him a glass.

Her fingers grazed against his as he took the glass from her. Unfamiliar heat and a strange tingling sensation flowed up her arm and through her body. Her breath hitched, and she jerked her hand away from his touch.

Had he noticed? Had he felt it, too? His glance didn't waver, but his eyes seemed to darken.

For a few minutes, they sat in silence, listening to the birds chirping in the trees beside the house, the perfume of the rose bushes filling the air.

"Nice garden," he said a little while later.

"I enjoy spending time planting and taking care of flowers."

Uncomfortable silence fell. Olivia couldn't remember ever being at a loss for words, and for the first time, her brain couldn't even make polite conversation. Thankfully, she saw Zane and Priscilla rounding the corner of the street. "Oh, good, there they are. And supper will be ready in a few minutes."

"I'm surprised they came," he said.

"I told you they would agree to come."

"You did, but I really didn't think they would."

Her gaze bored into his. "What would you have done if they hadn't come?"

"I would've left," he said. "I told you, I wouldn't risk you being gossiped about because of me."

Olivia smiled at him. "I appreciate that, but they are here. Does that make you feel better?"

"Yes and no."

"Why?"

"It might be awkward. Does that make sense?"

She nodded. "I'm sure it'll be fine."

She only hoped she was right.

The sun was a golden orb hovering over the peaks of the Rockies in the distance. Landry stood quietly on the porch while Zane, Priscilla and Olivia kept up a running conversation. Zane had been polite, but cool toward him. Priscilla, on the other hand, had been friendlier than he'd expected.

Still, he didn't belong here, and he wondered if there was some way he could escape without upsetting Olivia.

"Can you give me a hand setting the food out?" Olivia asked Priscilla, then turned to go inside.

Priscilla hurried behind Olivia, leaving Zane and Landry alone on the porch. Once the door closed behind them, Landry moved to the far end of the porch, looking out over the fields behind the house.

Zane straightened from his position leaning against the porch railing. "I'm guessing you're feeling a bit awkward right about now."

Landry turned to face him and nodded, but didn't answer.

"Olivia is important to me and Priscilla. I don't want to see her hurt."

"Understood."

"She told me you wouldn't come unless we came, too. That you didn't want to sully her reputation."

"That's right."

"That was good of you to think of that."

How was he supposed to respond to that? He couldn't think of anything to say, so he said nothing.

"You know, it wasn't easy for me and Priscilla at first either," Zane said. "You might not remember, but folks had plenty to say about the way she arrived in town. But eventually, she won them over and now, they've accepted her as if she'd grown up here. People will forget, but you have to give them time."

Landry nodded. He had no choice but to give them time and hope the sheriff was right.

"Supper's ready," Olivia said, appearing in the doorway.

Her cheeks were flushed, her eyes sparkling. The vision took Landry's breath away. She was beautiful, and sweet, and everything he'd ever wanted in a woman.

"Are you coming, Landry?" Olivia's voice slipped into his thoughts, and he realized he'd been staring.

"What ... oh ..."

Her scent wrapped him in lavender as he slipped past her and she followed him inside.

An hour later, Landry leaned back in his chair. "You're a fine cook, Olivia," he said, smiling.

"Thank you." A tinge of pink colored her cheeks.

Was she not used to compliments? The possibility surprised him. She was beautiful and kind, even if she was a bit pushy when it came to helping people who didn't want to be helped. But she obviously had a good heart, spending her time helping those less fortunate.

She got up and hurried into the kitchen, returning a minute later with an apple pie and a pitcher of cream.

Just as she set it on the table, a loud thump shook the door. She hurried and opened it. A boy she didn't recognize stood on the porch. "Is the sheriff here?" he asked Olivia, his voice panic-stricken.

Zane's chair scraped across the floor and he appeared in the doorway to the dining room and crossed to stand beside Olivia. "What is it?"

"You gotta come quick, Sheriff. There's a fight ... Lester Baines ... he ..." The boy leaned forward, bracing his hands on his thighs as he tried to catch his breath.

Before the boy finished his sentence, Zane grabbed his hat from the hook behind the door. "I'll be back as soon as I can," he called out, then bounded down the porch steps, the boy hurrying behind him as fast as his short legs could move.

Olivia stood at the door until Zane and the boy disappeared around the corner, then came back into the dining room and repeated what the boy had said. "I don't know anything more," she said. "Now please, let's finish dessert. There's nothing we can do, and I'm sure Zane will be back soon."

Although she set a slice of pie in front of each of them, it seemed their appetites had disappeared. Finally, Olivia got up to clear the table, but Priscilla took the plates out of her hand and put them back down. "Why don't you and

Landry go into the parlor or out onto the porch and talk for a little while? I'll wash up the dishes."

"Oh, no—"

Priscilla gave her a gentle shove. "You cooked. I'll clean up. I insist."

"All right then," Olivia said. "The porch?" she asked Landry.

He nodded.

Night had fallen while they were having their meals, and only a full moon illuminated their surroundings.

Her glance searched the shadows for Zane. "I hope there's not too much trouble ..." she murmured.

"Lester Baines has always been a troublemaker," Landry told her.

"I don't know him."

"You're better off that way. Lester and my brother were friends."

"And now?"

"Lester's still here and Tobias ... he just got out of prison a few weeks ago."

"Will he come back to Rocky Ridge?"

"I don't think so," Landry said. "He talked about heading down Texas way." He didn't add that even though he wanted his old life back, he was afraid that Tobias was too angry now to pick up the pieces. It made him sad to think that the bond they'd once shared was gone.

"You don't want to see him?" Olivia asked quietly. "I don't have any brothers or sisters, and I always thought how nice it would be to have family."

Landry shook his head. "I do, but I want the brother I used to have. He's not the same man now. I keep hoping he'll change back to the man he used to be, but I'm not sure he can."

"I'm sorry ..."

"None of it would have happened if Tobias hadn't ..." He let the rest of the words die on his tongue. "I'm not blaming him. It was my own fault for looking up to him, I suppose, and for trying to pay him back for what he'd done for me."

"What do you mean?"

He didn't answer for quite some time, trying to find the right words to explain what had happened. Olivia sat, waiting patiently, and he appreciated that.

He looked up at the night sky. The sight of those stars never got old, not since he'd spent so much time never seeing the sky.

"After my ma died, my pa took to the bottle. He was a mean drunk, and more times than not, it was Tobias that made sure I got fed. He made sure I had clean clothes to wear and that I went to school. He's the one who stood between me and my pa and took the beatings intended for me, too. So I looked up to him, wanted to be just like him."

Olivia rested her hand on his forearm, her gentle touch sending streaks of heat through him to settle low in his belly. He'd felt a woman's touch since he got out of prison, but never one that wrapped around his insides and made him feel ... soft. And ... cared about.

"But sometimes because you care about somebody, you ignore your gut instinct or accept things you shouldn't."

"If you'd rather not talk about it ..." Olivia began.

"I do want to. You know I've been in prison, and Zane likely told you why." He turned to face her. The lamplight gave her face a golden glow.

"He said you were convicted of robbing the bank."

"I was."

"Will you do it again?" she asked.

"No." The word came out strong and sure. That much he could guarantee.

She smiled up at him. "That's all I need to know."

"You're too trusting," he admonished her.

"I prefer to trust people until they give me reason not to rather than the other way around."

He used to think that way, too, until he'd found out the hard way that sometimes, trusting somebody could destroy your life. "It's easy to get hurt that way."

"I suppose that's true," she agreed, "but sometimes trust is all you can give someone."

A resigned sigh escaped his lips. Resigned because she was exactly the kind of woman he'd been looking for before he went to prison. And the kind of woman he didn't deserve now.

He wanted to kiss her. Wanted to feel her lips against his. Wanted to feel his arms around her, her softness against him.

What would she do if he kissed her? Would she slap him? Never speak to him again?

And what would *he* do if he kissed her? Would one kiss be enough? Or would it only make him want her more?

He shouldn't do it. He'd regret it. But he couldn't stop himself.

As if she sensed the war going on inside him, her lips parted, her eyes searching his. And if he wasn't wrong ...

He took a step closer, his hand reaching up to cradle her chin. For a moment, he didn't move, just took in the invitation in her eyes, then lowered his lips to hers. At the first touch of the softness of her lips, heat swept through his veins, settling low in his belly.

He kept the kiss as gentle as he could, sensing he might scare her if he deepened the kiss the way he was tempted to.

Lord, he wanted her. He'd never wanted a woman more. But she wasn't a saloon whore. She was a lady, a lady who was too good for him.

He released her lips and gazed down at her. Her eyes sparkled, her breath coming in short gasps. He glanced at her lips, desire like a whirlwind inside him.

"Landry?" Her voice was barely more than a whisper, but the invitation was clear. He swore, closing the gap, needing to feel her sweetness again more than he needed to breathe. He was lost!

Heavens! What was wrong with her?

The taste of Landry's lips intoxicated her. In the furthest recesses of her mind, she knew she should wrench herself out of his arms, should slap him for his boldness, and evict him from her house. And her life.

The night was warm and the lamp inside illuminated the porch. She breathed deeply, taking in the heavy perfume from the rosebushes growing near the porch.

And Landry's unique scent – soap, leather, male.

Eyes closed, she tilted her head, allowing Landry more access to her lips. Her curves molded to the hard planes of his chest, and she could feel his heart beating steadily through the thin fabric of her blouse.

His fingers grazed her throat, then wrapped her hair in his fist, the pressure of his lips on hers growing stronger. Her body tingled, heat and something she couldn't define surging through her limbs.

The sensation was so exquisite she wanted to stay like this all night. Forever.

Suddenly, his hands gripped her shoulders and eased her away from him. "I'm sorry," he whispered. "But I've been wanting to do that since the minute I saw you in that alley."

As much as she hated to admit it, she'd wanted it, too. And now that she'd tasted his lips, she wanted more. She wasn't exactly sure what 'more' was, only that something deep inside her craved it.

He placed another light kiss on her lips. "I have to go."

"Now? It's still early and—"

"I need to go. Right now." Turning, he bounded down the porch steps. As he disappeared into the night, the door opened.

Priscilla exited the house to stand beside her on the porch. "Landry left?" she asked.

Olivia nodded, wishing she knew what she'd done to send him hurrying away.

Chapter Five

Olivia studied the bags and cans on the shelf behind the counter in Todd's Mercantile the next morning. "A half pound of raisins and two pounds of sugar please."

Cammie Todd let out a laugh and shook her head good-naturedly. "I swear you go through more sugar than anyone else I know."

Olivia chuckled. She and Cammie had become friends when she'd joined Priscilla's knitting circle soon after Olivia had settled in Rocky Ridge. "You know how much I like to bake, and the children at the orphanage love it when I bring them treats. I planned to make cookies this afternoon but I didn't have enough raisins."

"You spoil those children," Cammie commented, filling a scoop with sugar and pouring it into a paper bag. She set it on the scale beside her and watched the dial until it stopped, then added more until it registered two pounds. "I wonder if you'll spoil your own children as much when you have them."

Olivia's smile faded. Having grown up as an only child, she'd always hoped for a large family one day. But time was running out. Even though she knew of two gentlemen in town who were interested in courting her, she couldn't imagine marrying for anything less than true love.

Not only did she have no romantic feelings for either of the two men, until a few days ago, she hadn't met even one man in town who stirred any emotion in her at all.

"Anything else I can get for you?" Cammie asked.

Olivia shook her head. "Not today, thanks."

A few minutes later, Olivia left the mercantile, her basket over her arm.

She'd stopped to admire a bonnet in the milliner's window when she saw caught sight of Mrs. Lundstrom, the town busybody, out of the corner of her eye.

As if Olivia had a bullseye on her back, Mrs. Lundstrom hurried toward her. "Good afternoon, Olivia," she said. "How are you? I haven't seen you since that unfortunate incident the other day."

Olivia returned her greeting. "I'm fine, thank you."

"I couldn't believe my ears when I heard what happened. Why, this town is going to ruin."

"I also heard that ..." Her voice lowered to a whisper and she slid a glance to the side, checking to make sure no one was within earshot. "That ex-convict saved you. How fortunate for you that he just happened to be nearby."

Sarcasm laced Mrs. Lundstrom's voice. Did she think Landry had something to do with it?

"It was very fortunate." Olivia met her glance steadily. "If Mr. Mitchell hadn't happened to be there, I don't like to think about what would have happened."

"What was he doing there anyway? The livery is at the other end of town. Unless the two of them were friends ..."

Knowing Mrs. Lundstrom's reputation for being the biggest gossip in town, Olivia was well aware she had to be careful with any information she offered. Still, what had happened was common knowledge, and it surprised her Mrs. Lundstrom hadn't already made a point of digging out every detail. Or perhaps she had, and she was hoping for a juicy tidbit that no one else knew.

"I see ...", Mrs. Lundstrom said once Olivia explained why Landry was close by when she was attacked, "but you do realize those kinds of people ... I wouldn't believe everything you hear ..."

Olivia plastered a smile on her lips. "Oh, believe me, Mrs. Lundstrom, I don't."

"Terrible what this world is coming to," Mrs. Lundstrom muttered. "A man like him walking around free as a bird among decent God-fearing people ..."

Olivia couldn't listen to her any longer. Normally, she hated any kind of gossip, but in this case ... A tiny smile creased her lips.

"But did you hear about what he did yesterday?"

"Who?"

"Mr. Mitchell."

Mrs. Lundstrom's lips pursed and a frown creased her forehead. "Why no, I didn't. What did he do?"

At supper the night before, Zane had asked

Landry if it was true that he'd helped Mr. Mooney repair his roof. Landry had seemed uncomfortable talking about it, but finally admitted he had. Then he'd quickly changed the subject.

Olivia described what had happened, taking her time, all the while knowing whatever she said would spread like wildfire.

"I'm sure he had an ulterior motive," Mrs. Lundstrom pointed out when she was done.

"I'm sure you're right. He was likely being a good neighbor by trying to prevent Mr. Mooney from injuring himself."

"Hmmph," Mrs. Lundstrom sputtered. "Well, dear, you're young and naïve. Mark my words, he's up to no good."

Olivia bristled. It was people like Mrs. Lundstrom who made it impossible for anyone to get past their mistakes and move on. "Thank you for your concern, Mrs. Lundstrom, but I do my best to forgive, as the Bible says we should. Now I'm sorry I don't have time to talk more. I really must hurry. Good day."

Before the woman had a chance to respond, Olivia hurried away. She didn't trust herself not to say something she might regret. Anger rushed through her. The woman was insufferable, but for once, her gossip might be helpful.

The Lucky Shamrock was full when Landry wandered in once he'd taken care of his evening chores and closed the main door to the livery for the night.

He'd been busier than usual that day. He didn't know why, but he wasn't about to question it. Even the new dentist in town had stopped by to ask him to look at the wheel on his buggy.

Landry sidled his way to the bar, rested one booted foot on the rail, and said, "Beer," in answer to the bartender's questioning glance.

Ansel opened the spigot and filled and glass, then slid it down the smooth surface of the bar before he moved away to tend to another customer.

Landry lifted it to his lips and took a long swallow. The liquid cooled his mouth, his insides warming as he swallowed and it flowed down.

He needed sleep, and he hoped that exhaustion from working more than twelve hours straight and the beer would be enough to keep thoughts of Olivia out of his mind long enough that he could get some shuteye.

He never should have gone to church, never should have agreed to have supper with her, and he definitely never should have kissed her.

One of the biggest mistakes you've ever made, Mitchell, he chastised himself. Some things couldn't be undone, and the memory of the warmth of her lips on his was one of them.

A voice calling his name drew his attention. He turned. Four men sat at a table, a deck of playing cards in the center. He recognized two of the men as hands from one of the ranches outside of town.

"Got an empty seat here," a ranch hand he knew only as Reese said. "Want to sit in?"

He didn't. All he wanted to do was finish his beer land head back to the livery to sleep. But this was the first time anybody had asked him to play poker since he got back. If he ever wanted to get his life back, it wouldn't be a good idea to refuse.

"Thanks." Picking up his glass, he jostled his way to the table and sat down.

"I'm out," he said two hours later. He drained his beer, then scooped up a few coins off the table. "Thanks for the game."

He got up, said goodnight and left the saloon. The air was cool and fresh after the smoke in the saloon, and for the first time since he'd come back to town, he thought he might still have a chance to turn things around.

"We have to do something for the children," Olivia said to Almira a few mornings later as they chopped vegetables in the orphanage kitchen. "I've never seen them misbehave so badly."

Almira set down her knife and began kneading her hand. Olivia couldn't help but notice the older woman's enlarged knuckles and misshapen fingers. Rheumatism, she'd told Olivia once. It bothered her in damp weather.

"It's the rain." Almira's glance strayed to the large window overlooking the gardens. "They haven't been able to get outside to run around, and the only way for them to use up their energy is to fight with each other."

It had been raining for what seemed like forever, and looking at the slate gray sky outside, it seemed it was never going to stop. Olivia had been feeling out of sorts herself, but she suspected it had more to do with the way Landry had left right after kissing her senseless than the weather.

She hadn't been able to rid her thoughts of him since that night, and he'd even started invading her dreams – dreams of him holding her, kissing her, touching her.

Almira's voice startled her out of her wicked thoughts. "Are you all right, dear? You seem a bit flushed. This weather—"

Olivia spun around to face the older woman, her face flushing with heat. "Oh ... yes ... I'm fine ..."

Heavens! She really needed to put Landry out of her mind. It was a kiss. Nothing more. She'd been kissed before, but she'd never had a kiss that made her insides turn into jelly.

Stop it! she scolded herself. Think about something else. Something warm and sunny and enjoyable ... Suddenly, it came to her. "Perhaps once the rain stops – if it ever does – we could arrange a picnic to the mill pond. What do you think?"

Almira paused in her ministrations to her hands. "You'll have these children so spoiled ..."

"I know," Olivia said, smiling, "but they need a bit of spoiling, don't you think? After what they've all been through? Losing their families in one way or another through no fault of their own ...?"

"You're right, of course." Almira picked up the knife and resumed chopping. "But I'm really too busy to plan a picnic—"

"I'll do it." Arranging a picnic would at least keep her occupied so she wouldn't spend her time thinking about a man who obviously regretted kissing her so much he'd practically run out of her house and she hadn't seen him since.

"I don't think that's a good idea," Almira put in. "I appreciate the offer, but there are too many obstacles."

Olivia glanced through the open doorway to the parlor where a few of the children were playing a game. Charity Quigg twirled one of her ringlets in her fingers as she looked at a picture book open on her lap. Daniel sat beside her, staring into space.

She wasn't sure why she was particularly drawn to Daniel. Could it be because she'd been there when he first arrived? All the other children had been there long before Olivia came to help, so she hadn't seen the adjustment they'd had to make. Or was it simply because he reminded her of how lonely she'd been as a child? Whatever the reason, her heart had gone out to him.

"If I can arrange it to your satisfaction," Olivia pressed, turning her attention back to Almira, "will you give me your permission?"

Almira scooped up a handful of carrots and added them to the large pot on the stove. "I will, but only because I know you'll keep after me until I give in." She chuckled. "I hope you can work out the details. The children would be thrilled."

Olivia couldn't prevent the excitement bubbling up inside her. Surprises for the children always gave her as much pleasure as it did them.

"First, transportation," she said, mostly to herself. Then, pausing in her chopping, she peered at Almira. "I saw a wagon in the shed a few weeks ago. Is it—?"

Almira shook her head. "The axle's broken. Mr. Cruickshank at the livery promised to fix it, but he sold out before he got around to it."

"That's not a problem. Landry can fix it."

Almira looked away, her glance focused on stirring the vegetables in the pot. "I ... I'd rather not …"

"I beg your pardon?"

"Now I understand how you feel about giving the man a second chance, but—"

"He's trying, Almira," Olivia pointed out. "And you did leave it up to me to make the arrangements."

"We can't afford to fix the wagon—"

"I'll pay for it." Olivia put down her knife and slid the remaining carrots into the pot. "Any other objections?"

Almira opened her mouth as if she wanted to say more, but closed it again and shook her head.

"Good," Olivia said. "Now if you'll excuse me, I have plans to make."

And first on her list was a visit to Landry.

Olivia picked her way through the puddles and rain-filled wagon ruts outside the livery. The steady downpour had finally died down to a misty drizzle, and she hurried as quickly as she could to shelter.

At the entrance to the livery, she lowered her umbrella and shook off the water, then leaned it against the wall.

She waited at the doorway until her eyes grew accustomed to the dim light inside, then stepped farther into the building. Landry obviously hadn't heard her enter, his concentration on the piece of metal he was hammering at the anvil. She couldn't resist just watching him work. He'd removed his shirt, and she was mesmerized by the play of muscles beneath his skin as he moved. An unfamiliar sensation as if warm liquid was flowing through her veins overtook her, and her heartbeat quickened. As she watched, he picked the piece of metal up with a pair of tongs and moved it to the forge. The flames cast a glow on his skin, giving it a look of polished bronze.

As if he sensed her presence, he glanced toward her, and a slow smile spread across his face. "Afternoon, Olivia," he said, his voice washing over her like a caress.

Taking in a calming breath, she returned his greeting. Was it too forward for her to mention the way he'd left so abruptly after supper? Should she wait to see if he brought it up?

"Give me a minute to finish this." He continued to work, taking the metal out of the flames and placing it on the anvil, then hammering it into shape. Then he dipped it in a bucket of water. A loud hiss and cloud of steam filled the air. "Why are you out in the rain?" he asked when he'd lifted the metal bar out of the water and set it on a long worktable. "You'll catch your death."

She could tell him the truth, that she couldn't stand to wait one more day to see him again. Yes, she had a valid reason for making the trip to the livery, and if Mr. Cruickshank still owned it, she likely would have waited until the rain stopped. But she wanted ... no, she needed ... to see him. "I ... I want to hire you."

He picked up a cloth and wiped his hands, then moved toward her. A sheen of perspiration covered his bare chest, and her breath hitched in her throat.

A slow smile lifted his lips as he stopped and crossed his arms. "You do? What for?"

"The axle on the wagon at the orphanage is broken. I need to have it fixed. You can do that, can't you?"

"I didn't even know the orphanage had a wagon."

"It's been in the shed for years, from what I've been told."

"So why the hurry to get it fixed now?"

Olivia couldn't keep the excitement out of her voice as she outlined her plan to take the children on a picnic at the pond.

When she was finished, he studied her for a moment then shook his head in confusion. "Either you're the most generous person I've ever met or the dumbest."

Olivia bristled. "Dumb? Why ever would you say I'm dumb?"

"Why do you do it? What do you get out of it?"

"Do what? My work at the orphanage?"

He nodded.

"I do it because those children need someone who cares about them. They need to be able to go to sleep at night knowing they're safe, and that they won't go hungry."

"So you spend your days doing for everybody else, never expecting anybody to do anything for you."

She supposed that was true. But she didn't need anyone's help. She was managing fine. Her grandfather had bequeathed her the house she lived in and a small allowance. As long as she didn't spend extravagantly, she'd have everything she needed for the rest of her life. If only she also had everything she'd ever wanted.

She had no husband, no children of her own, and until recently no one who really cared if she lived or died. Now, because she'd made a point of becoming indispensable to the orphanage as well as helping anyone else in town who was in distress, she mattered to them. People cared about her.

"I don't need anyone to do anything for me," she pointed out. "I'm quite capable of looking after myself. It's not foolishness, Landry. I enjoy helping those less fortunate than I am, and I don't expect reward. My reward is how it makes me feel."

"How does it make you feel?" he asked.

"It gives me pleasure. Knowing I've made a difference in someone's life is all the reward I need. How did it make you feel to help Mr. Mooney with his roof?"

"That's different," he countered. "He's far too old to go scrambling around on a roof. He was going to get himself killed. I was just—"

"Helping without expecting anything in return, and did it not give you a warm feeling inside?"

He shrugged. "I suppose so ..." he finally admitted.

"And that's why I do what I do," she said, smiling. "Now, about the axle ..."

"I'll ride over there as soon as I can and see what I can do."

"Thank you."

Her business was finished, yet she found herself reluctant to leave. She'd enjoyed spending time with him. But she should leave. She knew that, but couldn't tear herself away. Finally, he took a step toward her.

"Look, Olivia," he began, "about the other night ... I was wrong ... I shouldn't have ..." His voice trailed off, and he looked away, as if he couldn't face her.

Her heart squeezed. She couldn't bear to hear the apology, to know their kiss had meant nothing to him when it had had such a profound effect on her. She held her hand up to stop him. "Please don't give it another thought."

"But—"

Her throat tightened and her eyes burned. "Really. It was just a kiss. Now I really must go." Before it was too late and he saw the tears streaming down her cheeks.

She spun around and, mindless of the puddles, hurried away as quickly as she could away to get home. Only there could she let her tears fall as they may.

Landry watched her go, her feet splashing in the puddles, the hem of her skirt dragging through the mud. What had he said that had made her so skittish? He shook his head. He'd never understand women.

Ever since he'd made the mistake of kissing her, he'd barely been able to function, which explained the four ruined horseshoes lying on the workbench near the back of the livery.

Olivia's face filled his mind whenever he closed his eyes to sleep, and more times than not he'd had to get up and douse himself with ice-cold water to cool his heated blood.

He'd wanted to go to her, to apologize, but

staying away from her had seemed like the smartest thing to do.

And then she'd shown up, her bright eyes seeing right through to his soul. He'd tried to tell her how sorry he was, that he knew he had no business kissing her like that.

But hell, that kiss … The touch of her lips on his had made him want to do far more than just kiss her, while at the same time, made him want to do nothing more than just hold her close, breathe in her scent, and savor her warmth.

And he got the feeling she felt the same way.

But he couldn't have her. He didn't deserve her.

It did seem like over the past few days, he'd made a start rebuilding his life. The new schoolteacher had bid him a good afternoon when he'd passed her on the street the day before. Two elderly men he recognized as friends of his father's looked up from their checker game in front of the feed store and gave him a half wave. And being invited to join the poker game was definitely a step in the right direction, even though he didn't plan to spend his nights in The Lucky Shamrock.

Maybe, with enough time, people would accept him again. And then … then he'd tell Olivia how he felt.

A slow smile tugged at his lips at the thought that one of these days, he might get the chance to kiss Olivia again. But until then, he'd have to do his best to avoid her. That would be hard to do since he'd already agreed to fix the wagon at the orphanage, but it would be easy enough to find out her schedule and make sure he stayed away when she was there.

With that decision made, he went back to work. He was hammering a plow blade into shape an hour later when voices behind him made him turn around.

His eyes widened, and a broad smile lifted his lips.

Chapter Six

"Tobias!"

The last time they'd spoken was the day Landry had been released from prison. Tobias had told him he was going to Texas. So what was he doing back in Rocky Ridge?

"Hey, little brother," Tobias said. "Aren't you a sight for sore eyes?" He swaggered into the livery, his thumbs hooked into the gunbelt hanging low on his hips.

"Same goes for you." Landry rounded the workbench and crossed to meet him, the hammer he'd been using still in his hand. He took a long look at his brother, taking in the changes since they'd last seen each other. "It's real good to see you."

Tobias took off his hat and held it at his side. His dark hair was thinner and shaggy now, hanging to his shoulders. He was leaner than he used to be, too, his cheekbones more pronounced and barely more than skin covering bone. Deep lines furrowed beside his mouth. And there was a hardness about him Landry had never noticed before. Even his eyes looked empty, cold.

Tobias rested his hip against the table where Landry had been working. A cheroot dangled out of the corner of his mouth, the ashes dangerously close to falling off.

Landry eyed the glowing end of the cigarillo. "Mind taking that thing outside before you set the place on fire?"

For a few seconds, Landry thought Tobias was going to ignore him, but finally his brother moved to the door and flicked the cigarillo into the yard. It sputtered and died in the mud.

Landry set the hammer down on the table. "How are you doing?"

"Good now."

"Where've you been? I thought you were heading down Texas way once you got out."

Tobias shrugged. "Around. Here and there. I'm thinking about heading south, but wanted to stop by and see my little brother before I left. Can't tell you how surprised I was when I heard you were back here. And a business owner, too."

"It's where I want to be."

Tobias nodded, but Landry doubted he really understood. Then Tobias moved away, wandering through the livery, picking up tools and setting them back down.

"You really think folks want you here? I'd wager they'd be happy if you left and never came back."

Landry couldn't dispute Tobias's reasoning. He'd thought the same thing since the day he'd ridden back into town. Lately, though, he'd started to think maybe there might be a chance. And that was all due to one person – Olivia Harding.

A faint smile tugged at his lips. The majority

of the townsfolk might want him gone, but there was one woman he was pretty sure wanted him to stay.

"Where are you staying?" Landry asked.

"Me and the boys are camped outside town."

A sliver of unease snaked up Landry's spine. Surely he wasn't back running with the men who'd gotten him into trouble in the first place. "Boys?"

"Gage and Uggie."

A lead weight settled in Landry's stomach. "Is that a good idea? Look what happened last time you got mixed up with them."

Tobias closed the gap between them. Even though Landry was a few inches taller than Tobias, the hardened expression on his brother's face made him feel like a little boy again. "If it wasn't for them, you wouldn't have had such an easy time growing up."

That much was probably true, although at the time, he hadn't given much thought to where Tobias got the money to provide for them both after their mother died.

"Me and the boys have got some business to take care of before we head south, but I didn't want to leave without asking you to come with us."

Something in the tone of Tobias's voice sent a chill through Landry. "What kind of business?"

"I'll let you know once everything's in place."

Tobias was up to something. Landry was sure of it. But what? And why would Tobias think Landry wanted any part of it?

"I don't need to know," Landry told him. "Doesn't concern me. I'm putting my life back together—"

Tobias let out a bitter laugh and waved his arm to take in the livery. "This is what you call a life? Hell, boy, I raised you to want more out of life than this."

"You did, Tobias. And I'm grateful. But I spent three years in prison because of you and your friends—"

"I tried to tell them. We all tried to tell them."

"I know that, but they didn't' listen. I don't know what you're planning, but I'm not willing to spend one more day behind bars."

"You won't. This time—"

Landry raised his hand to stop his brother saying anything more. "No. No more. You do what you want to do, but don't include me. I have plans of my own."

"Like what?"

"Like being part of a community again. Like maybe finding me a woman and settling down, raising a family. Like growing old without having to look over my shoulder or having people treat me like dirt."

"Wouldn't you rather have enough money to buy anything you want without scraping by for scraps? You can buy yourself a woman. As for settling down and raising a few brats ... Just think about it." Straightening, Tobias turned and walked away.

Landry watched him go, his mind in turmoil. Sure, he'd made it sound as if it was easy to fit back into town as if he'd never been gone, but they both knew it was a lie.

When he'd decided to come back to Rocky Ridge, he'd wanted his old life back, wanted his old friends back, wanted forgiveness and acceptance.

But that hadn't happened, and there were times he wondered why he was even trying.

Now, with Tobias back, it would be easy to fall back into old habits, to follow Tobias the way he had his whole life until that night ... the night that had changed his life.

The summer sun warmed Olivia as she knelt in the garden outside the orphanage. She'd taken over looking after the garden the summer before, and this year, it looked like they'd be able to harvest enough berries and vegetables to last them for months. Anywhere the orphanage could save a few dollars was worth a little extra effort.

She'd planned to stay home that afternoon, but since the rain had stopped, she'd decided to take the opportunity to pull the weeds while the soil was still damp.

Resting back on her heels for a moment, she glanced up at the wispy clouds floating in the clear blue sky. An absolutely perfect day, she mused.

The rattle of harness from the front of the house caught her attention. Since Almira was at the mercantile stocking up on supplies and the older children were inside doing lessons, Olivia stood up and removed her work gloves, then draped them over the rim of the bucket holding the weeds she'd already pulled.

Brushing her skirt, she hurried around the side of the house to see who their visitor was. She stopped short when she saw Landry climbing the steps to the front porch.

Her heart leaped into her throat. She didn't

want to see him, wasn't prepared to deal with him, but she had no choice if she wanted their wagon axle repaired.

And having the wagon to use for the picnic was more important than her feelings.

Taking in a few calming breaths, she forced his name past the tightness in her throat. "Landry."

He turned at the mention of his name, his eyes widening when he saw her. Climbing back down the porch steps, he stopped in front of her. "Afternoon, Olivia. I didn't expect to see you here."

He seemed uncomfortable, even nervous, yet why he would be, she didn't know. "Is that why you came today?"

"Of course not," he said. "This is the first chance I've had."

"I see," she said softly. Still, something made her wonder if he was telling the truth - the way he was avoiding her gaze, his hands clenching and unclenching, shifting from one foot to the other as if he was unable to stand in one spot.

"Where's the wagon you need fixed?" he asked finally.

She pointed to a long weathered building at the far edge of the property. "In the shed. I'll show you."

In silence, they walked around the side of the house. He stopped when he saw the garden. "Is that what you were doing?" he asked, his glance drifting over her soil-stained apron and mud-covered boots.

She nodded. "I enjoy it, and it means we

don't have to buy fresh fruits and vegetables."

"That's true."

"Come with me," she said. She took a few steps, then realizing he was walking behind her, stopped until he caught up. It made her feel uncomfortable knowing he was watching her walk. When they reached the shed, she tugged the door open and stepped inside.

Stale air and dust met her nose. "Here it is," she said, then stepped aside so Landry could take a closer look.

The wagon was old, the blue paint peeled and blistered to reveal cracked weathered wood underneath. It listed to one side where the spokes from one of the wheels were broken or missing. The rusted metal rim lay on the dirt beside the wheel.

As he moved past her in the small space, he brushed against her. Her heart raced, and her skin tingled at his nearness. For a few moments, he paused. Their eyes met, and she found herself holding her breath.

His heated glance bore into her. The air between them sizzled. She shouldn't want him to kiss her, but Lord help her, she did. At that moment, she wanted to feel his lips on hers and his arms around her more than she'd ever wanted anything.

The moment passed. He moved away, and even though the shed was stifling hot, a chill filled her.

Landry slowly made his way around the entire wagon, stopping every few seconds to examine something. He tugged at the wagon tongue and a moment later, the rusty pin attaching the tongue to the wagon box fell out.

"Can you fix it?" she asked. If it was beyond repair, taking the children on a picnic would be impossible.

"It's in pretty bad shape," he commented.

She nodded. "Almira told me it hasn't been used in years, but I hoped it wouldn't take much to make it usable. Can you fix it? I so hope you can. I can't wait to tell the children—"

A smile creased his lips. He chuckled. "Do you always get like this when you're planning a surprise?"

"Like what?"

"Like you're about to bust out of your skin?"

Her face flushed. She couldn't help herself. "I'm afraid so."

"It's nice," he murmured.

"It is?"

He nodded. "But do you ever do anything nice for yourself?"

"Why ... of course ..."

"Like what?"

"Well ..." She paused, trying to come up with something, anything, she'd done for herself to make her life easier or more enjoyable."

"I thought so," he said. "Seems everything you do is for other people. Not that it's a bad thing. It's nice to see there are still people in this world who aren't just out for themselves. But maybe once in a while you should take some time to be nice to yourself."

He didn't understand. Couldn't understand that by being a good neighbor, by helping other people, she *was* being nice to herself She had no husband to care for, no children to love. Doing for others was the only thing that made her feel worthwhile, needed.

She couldn't explain why it was so important to her to feel needed, and she suspected if she continued this conversation, his questions would become more personal, questions she couldn't answer. "So, can you fix the wagon?"

He folded his arms across his chest as he stood and stared at the wagon for quite some time before he answered. "I could," he said finally, "but it's not worth fixing. I'd almost have to rebuild the whole thing."

Olivia's heart sank. She'd really hoped the wagon was in better shape than it looked. But, at least the children wouldn't be disappointed, she consoled herself. "Oh ... well, thank you for letting me know."

"You're welcome." He stepped outside, and Olivia followed.

The pine-scented air was a welcome respite from the stuffiness inside the shed, and she took a deep cleansing breath.

"Look," he said, pausing near the garden. "It's a shame that the children won't get their picnic, so you're welcome to use my wagon if you want."

"Really?" Her excitement began to build again. "Are you sure?"

He nodded. "I don't use it much, just if I have to cart something from one of the ranches into town to fix."

"Then I accept, with thanks."

"Fine. Just let me know when."

Together, they rounded the side of the house. Suddenly, she froze, her hand automatically reaching out and grabbing Landry's arm when she saw Daniel standing beside the horse tied to the back of Landry's wagon.

Fear surged through her. Daniel was so small, and the caramel-colored horse was so huge. Yet as she watched, Daniel reached up and ran his hand gently down the animal's neck. The horse nickered. Daniel stopped, and the horse turned its head and nudged him. Daniel smiled.

"What's the matter?" Landry asked.

Emotion choked her. "It's ... it's the first time I've seen Daniel without a frown."

"Is that so?"

For a few minutes, they waited, watching the little boy befriend the horse before they crossed the yard.

"Daniel?" she said softly.

The boy's eyes widened when he saw them. His smile disappeared, guilt washing across his face.

"My name's Landry Mitchell," Landry said, holding out his hand. "I'm happy to meet you. And since Chester's decided you're his friend, that means we'll be friends, too."

Daniel stared up at him for a few seconds, then hesitantly reached out and let his small hand be buried in Landry's.

"This is Chester," Landry told him, rubbing the horse's head. "Do you like him?"

Daniel nodded.

"Do you know how to ride?"

He nodded again.

Olivia wasn't surprised. Daniel's parents had owned a farm so it was likely they'd taught the boy to ride.

"Would you like to ride him sometime?"

Interest sparked in Daniel's eyes. With his glance glued to Landry, his face lit up in a grin. "Yes, sir."

Olivia sucked in a breath. Daniel had finally spoken.

Chapter Seven

Olivia glanced up at the sky. She couldn't have asked for a more perfect day for a picnic.

"Hurry, children. We're wasting time," she said as they gathered at the bottom of the stairs. "Mr. Mitchell has been kind enough to lend us a wagon, and we don't want to make him wait. So everyone carry something and let's go."

A few minutes later, the picnic baskets they'd packed earlier were stowed in the wagon bed. The children were huddled together beside them, and Landry was sitting on the bench, his hand reaching to help Olivia up into the wagon.

A tingle seeped through her and settled low in her stomach as his work-roughened fingers closed around hers. "Thank you," she murmured as she sat beside him. Their thighs met, his heat seeping through the fabric of her dress and petticoats. Her breath hitched in her throat.

"You sure you can handle the wagon yourself?" he asked as they slowly made their way down Rocky Ridge's main street toward the livery.

"Of course," she assured him.

He slid a glance at her. "You look real pretty

today."

"Thank you." Her cheeks pinked. She had to admit she'd taken pains with her appearance, knowing she'd see Landry and hoping he'd find her attractive. After going through her wardrobe, she'd finally settled on a pale yellow dress patterned with tiny flowers and trimmed with white lace. She'd had compliments when she'd worn that dress before, so she knew it was becoming on her. She'd also taken the time to curl her hair, pinning it on her head and leaving a few tendrils to frame her face.

The children chattered behind them, making it unnecessary for Olivia and Landry to carry on a conversation. Finally, Landry did break the silence between them. "You're taking the children yourself?"

She nodded. "Mrs. Potts decided to stay behind with the babies and the young ones."

"I see. You sure you can handle them all yourself?"

She wasn't sure, but she hoped the older children would help her with the younger ones. The children had all promised they'd be on their best behavior, and she had threatened that if one of them misbehaved, the picnic would be over and she'd immediately take them home. She hoped that would be enough. "We'll see," she said, giving him a hopeful smile.

"You can let me off at the livery," he said. "Just bring the wagon back whenever you're done with it."

Olivia nodded, but disappointment filled her. She'd wondered if he might offer to join them, but apparently he had no interest in spending the day with a horde of children.

A minute or so later, they reached the livery. Landry pulled on the reins and handed them to her.

"Thank you again for lending us the wagon," she said. "Are you very busy today?"

"Not particularly," he responded. "Why?"

Should she? Her teeth worried her bottom lip for a few moments as propriety warred with desire inside her. Desire won. "Would you like to come with us?"

Lines formed between his brows. "You mean on your picnic?"

She nodded. "I'm sure the boys would enjoy having you there."

"What about the woman? Would she enjoy having me there, too?"

How was she supposed to answer that? She could lie and say she had no preference either way, but she'd never been good at masking her feelings. Yet admitting she wanted to spend time with him was highly improper. Then again, being proper had never gotten her anywhere. "She would," she said quietly, smiling. "Very much."

Their gazes locked but he didn't speak for a few moments. "I didn't want to intrude, but if I'm invited ..." Then he reached over, smiled and took the reins back out of her hands.

The older children's' squeals and laughter rang through the quiet meadow surrounding the mill pond. Two of the younger children were sleeping on blankets beneath the shade of a weeping willow. Olivia and Landry sat on a blanket beside them, keeping an eye on the older children in the pond. Three girls sat nearby, playing with rag dolls.

She smiled at the children jumping off the bank into the pond, pleased she could give them a day of enjoyment rather than the humdrum existence they usually led at the orphanage.

Almira had a set schedule for everything from mealtimes to baths to lessons and playtime. Today was the first time since she'd started helping out at the orphanage that the schedule had varied.

She cast a glance at Landry. He was sitting at the base of the tree where she'd spread a blanket, his back resting against the trunk. His gaze was focused on the children in the pond, and she was grateful to have an extra pair of eyes to watch over the children as they swam.

A faint smile quirked his lips, the tiny lines at the corners of his eyes crinkling. Olivia had never been partial to men with facial hair, but somehow, the dark stubble shadowing Landry's jaw only made him even more handsome.

As if he sensed her eyes on him, he turned and met her gaze. Olivia's heart skittered in her chest at the raw desire in his eyes. She forgot to breathe.

"Whatcha doin', Mr. Mitchell?"

Olivia started. She'd been so caught up in Landry's heated glance she hadn't even noticed Daniel approaching. She'd been sure Landry was about to kiss her. And what was worse, she was about to let him. With children watching! Heaven's, what was she thinking?

Landry grinned at the little boy. "Just sitting, Daniel. Enjoying the sunshine. Why aren't you in the water? You don't like swimming?"

He shook his head, then dropped onto the blanket beside Landry. He squirmed until his back was against the tree, his ankles crossed, his arms folded across his chest, exactly the way Landry's were.

"What do you like to do, Daniel?" Landry asked.

Daniel shrugged. "I like to plant things like my Pa did."

Strange, Olivia thought, he'd never shown any interest in the garden at the orphanage. "You're welcome to help me whenever you'd like," she told him.

He shook his head but didn't answer.

"I used to like to plant things, too, when I was a boy," Landry said.

"Why don't you plant things now? You're a man so you get to do anything you want."

Landry chuckled. "I wish that were true, Daniel. Even when you're a man you can't do whatever you want to do."

"My ma always said ..." Daniel's voice trailed off, and he looked away, but not before Olivia noticed a brightness in his eyes that hadn't been there moments before.

"I'm going to check on the children swimming," Olivia said, getting up. "It's almost time to get back."

Olivia strolled down to the edge of the pond, adjusting her bonnet to shade her eyes. The sun beat down, and as she watched the children frolicking in the water, she was glad she'd been able to give them some enjoyment, at least for a few hours.

She glanced over her shoulder and caught Landry watching her. Heat stole over her and settled low inside her that had nothing to do with the sunshine. He smiled, and even though she was too far away, she could easily imagine how his eyes twinkled and tiny creases appeared at the corners of his eyes. Then he turned back to look at Daniel and nodded, lowering his head as they fell into a deep conversation.

A smile tugged at her lips. It looked like the two of them were forming a friendship, a bond that she was confident would help them both.

Landry couldn't remember ever feeling more comfortable with a woman. He'd never been lonely for a lady's company, but until the day he met Olivia, he hadn't realized what had been missing. He enjoyed spending time with women, enjoyed what they'd offered, but he'd never really *liked* a woman. Until now.

He liked Olivia. Liked her sweetness and her kindness, and even her stubbornness when she set her mind on something. She made him forget about the horror of being behind bars, and made him think about the future. And he liked looking at her, liked the freckles that dotted her nose, and the way her eyes changed from brown to gold depending on her mood. He liked her curves and the way her hips swayed when she walked, and the way she fit against him when he held her close, as if they were two parts of one whole.

But she also made him want things he wasn't sure he'd ever have now, like a real home. A wife. A family.

She would overlook his past, even though it would ruin her reputation. But he couldn't bring himself to be selfish enough to let her sacrifice the life she'd built here for him, no matter how much he wanted to. And the truth of it was, he wanted her. Beside him, and in his bed. He wanted to smell the lavender scent that filled his nose with every breath, wanted the soft yellow hair he itched to run his fingers through, wanted the creamy skin he ached to touch ...

Spending the afternoon with her was a mistake. He'd pay for it later, when her face filled his dreams and his body lusted to hold her and love her. But if he had to do it again, he knew he would.

"Thank you for spending so much time with Daniel this afternoon," she said quietly once they'd packed up all the remnants of their picnic and Landry was stowing them in the wagon bed. "He still doesn't speak to anyone, and although he does his chores, he doesn't spend time with any of the other children. It seems you're the only one who can break through his wall of silence."

"Maybe he knows I understand what it's like to be alone at that age."

"Were you? Alone, I mean?"

He nodded. "Might as well have been. My ma died when I was ten. Pa took to the bottle and we stayed out his way as much as we could until he died. Then there was nowhere for me and my brother to go, so we stayed at the farm. A few neighbors helped, showed us how to plant enough vegetables to keep us going for the winter. Tobias found work in town and made sure I was looked after and went to school."

"Oh my ..."

At the stricken expression on Olivia's face, Landry realized he'd said too much. He didn't want her sympathy. "It wasn't so bad. We got by, but then Tobias started staying out late, got caught up in things he shouldn't have. The sheriff tried to keep him out of trouble, and for a while, it looked like things would turn out okay—"

"But it didn't."

He shook his head. "He was running with a bad crowd, and when I found out they were planning to rob the bank in town, I tried to stop him."

"But you were involved, too?"

The memory rushed back as if it had happened the day before. "No, I wasn't. I'd tried to make him see sense, but he wasn't listening. So I followed him, still hoping I could change his mind. By the time I got there, it was too late. They were just coming out of the bank. Right then, the sheriff and his deputy showed up. Two of the men were killed, and Tobias and me were arrested."

"But if you weren't involved—"

"Tobias and his cohorts tried to tell them I was innocent. A few of the townsfolk told the sheriff I wasn't there so he did his best to convince the judge, but he didn't believe any of them."

"So you went to prison."

"That's right."

"Then why hasn't the town accepted you back?" she asked.

"A few have, but some people still think I was guilty. Emmett for one."

"That's why he acted the way he did the night I was attacked."

He nodded. "Seems like I've made a lot of mistakes in my life and there's no going back to fix them. Sometimes you have to just accept the way it is and make the best of it."

Olivia rested a hand on his arm, her warmth surging through him. The biggest mistake of his life was standing right beside him.

"He'd fly through the air with the greatest of ease, That daring young man on the flying trapeze ..."

Olivia smiled at the children's off-key voices as they sang – loudly – during the ride along the trail toward town.

It had been a wonderful afternoon. She suspected she had enjoyed it even more than the children had. And that was because of Landry.

He was so easy to talk to, while at the same time, he evoked emotions and sensations that made her feel more alive than she ever had.

Her heart ached for the injustice done to him by the law and some of the town's residents. Surely they couldn't still believe he'd taken part in the robbery when witnesses testified they'd seen him arrive after it was over.

But there would always be those who wanted to think the worst of people – Emmett and Mrs. Lundstrom, for instance. She doubted they had a good word to say about anyone. Yet they seemed to be able to influence others to their way of thinking.

"A penny for your thoughts," Landry said quietly.

She chuckled. "I was thinking about what a

lovely day it's been. I can't thank you enough for everything."

"No need to thank me," he said. "I had a good time."

Had he really enjoyed it, or was he merely being polite?

His dark glance bored into hers, stealing her breath. The way he looked at her sometimes stirred up sensations she didn't understand. Heat, a strange sensation deep in her core, a tingle that seemed to spread through her from her head to the tips of her toes.

She tore her glance away and focused on the scenery. Brightly-colored wildflowers dotted the meadows on either side of the trail, while giant pine, spruce and fir trees stretched to the clear blue sky. In the distance, snow still clung to the mountain peaks. The sun hung low in the sky, the air growing cooler.

They'd travelled only a few miles when three riders rounded a bend in the trail. Olivia noticed Landry's fingers tighten on the reins. She raised her eyes to his face. A muscle tightened in his jaw, and he straightened his back, his body taut with tension.

The children, sensing the change in the mood, stopped singing and sat quietly in the wagon bed.

Landry drew on the reins when the three men blocked their path.

Olivia didn't speak, a cold chill washing over her. Something in their eyes made her uneasy.

"Afternoon, Landry," the tallest man said, urging his horse closer to the side of the wagon.

"Afternoon." The word came out clipped.

"You remember Uggie and Gage."

"How could I forget?"

"No need to be like that," Tobias said. He gave a cursory glance at the children in the wagon bed, then slid to Olivia. His glance raked over her. "Aren't you going to introduce me to your lady friend?"

Landry's lips thinned. "Olivia Harding, meet Tobias Mitchell. My brother."

Chapter Eight

The Lucky Shamrock was packed when Landry wandered in later that night. He hadn't seen Tobias and his friends since they'd met on the trail that afternoon and if he was being honest with himself, he was glad.

It made him sad that he wasn't happier to see his brother after their time apart. Tobias was the only family Landry had, and they'd been close growing up. It wasn't until Tobias had found new friends that their relationship had gotten strained.

Now, after spending so much time in prison, he'd changed and was unrecognizable as the brother he'd grown up with. Even though they were related by blood, they seemed to be more like old friends who'd lost touch over the years and had nothing to say to each other now.

"Over here."

Landry didn't need to turn around. He recognized Tobias's voice. He'd hoped to avoid him, but he should have known Tobias would be in the saloon. Where else would he go?

Waving an acknowledgement, he stopped at the bar and ordered beer, then made his way across the saloon to a table near the window.

Tobias and his friends were already well on the way to getting drunk and Uggie had one of the saloon girls on his lap.

She smiled at Landry as he slid into the vacant chair beside his brother. Uggie's arm was wrapped around the woman's waist so she couldn't leave even if she wanted to.

"This is Dolly," Uggie said, twirling one of the woman's ringlets in his finger and tugging until she was close enough he could plant a kiss on her neck. "Her and me are going to have us some fun tonight, aren't we, honey?"

Dolly smiled at Uggie, but it was obvious to Landry she wasn't looking forward to it. "Sure thing, cowboy."

Landry took a long swallow of beer, wishing he'd stayed back at the livery.

"So what's the story with the gal you were with this afternoon?" Tobias asked.

Landry bristled. He didn't want to talk about Olivia, especially to Tobias. And especially since he hadn't quite figured out himself exactly how strong his feelings were for her. All he knew was that when they were together, he felt ... different.

"She's quite a looker," Tobias put in without waiting for Landry to answer. "And got curves I wouldn't mind—"

"Shut up, Tobias." Landry had never stood up to his brother before, but he couldn't stand by and listen to him talking about Olivia as if she was a saloon whore. She was decent, respectable. And he cared about her. Hell, a lot more than he should. Enough that he wouldn't let anybody – even his brother – disrespect her.

The realization made him almost gasp aloud. He swore inwardly. He'd known better than to get involved with her. Known she was too good for him. But he'd gone ahead and done it anyway.

Tobias's voice interrupted his thoughts. "What? Since when is a woman good for anything but pleasuring a man? She sure looks like she could show me a good time."

"Leave her alone."

"You got a claim on her or something?" Tobias struck a match on the table and held it to the end of the cigarillo he'd put in his mouth. Smoke curled upward into the air.

"No."

"But you are sweet on her, aren't you? Well, well, well." Tobias grinned, but there was no warmth in his eyes. "But as long as she's not spoken for, she's fair game, don't you think so, boys?" he said, turning to his friends for agreement.

Gage and Uggie spoke up at the same time with their own version of Tobias's comments.

Fury like he'd never known before surged through Landry. He bounded up, the chair scraping against the wooden floor. The noise attracted the attention of a group of men playing poker at the next table. Out of the corner of his eye, Landry noticed them scrambling to get out of the way in case shooting started.

Landry moved until he towered over Tobias. His fists were clenched at his side. "Stay away from her, Tobias. I mean it. You go near her and ... I'll kill you."

Even as the words spilled from his mouth, he couldn't believe he was threatening his brother. It came as an even bigger shock to him that he meant every word. If Tobias laid one finger on Olivia …

Why did he care what woman caught Tobias's eye? Tobias was right. Landry had no claim on Olivia and whatever Tobias did with her was no business of his. So why did his stomach churn at the thought of the two of them together?

The temptation to wipe the smug expression off Tobias's face was almost overwhelming.

Tobias held up his hands in surrender. "Sure thing, little brother. If you want to keep her for yourself, that's fine with me. There's plenty of other women who'd be glad to keep me company. Ain't that right, Dolly?"

Dolly smiled, but didn't answer.

Landry and Tobias locked eyes for a few seconds. Tobias had seemed to back down. But what if he hadn't? A heaviness wrapped around Landry as it sank in that he was falling in love with Olivia and that he'd meant what he'd said to Tobias. If he laid one hand on Olivia, Landry would in fact kill his only brother.

"You Landry Mitchell?" a voice called out from behind him.

Turning, he saw a tall, rail-thin man shouldering his way past two cowboys loitering near the bar.

Some paused in their conversations to watch the man approaching Landry. Landry understood why. Now that the confrontation between Landry and Tobias seemed to have settled down, they were keeping an eye on the newcomer.

Landry had never seen the man before and he couldn't help wondering how he knew who he was. "Who's asking?"

The man stopped beside him and held out his hand. "Name's Josiah Mooney," he said.

Mooney, Landry thought. So this must be one of Curtis Mooney's kin.

"My pa's a stubborn old coot," Mooney said. "One of these days he's gonna get hisself killed. Can't admit he's not young enough to do everything for hisself. Just wanted to thank you."

Tobias came to stand beside Landry. "What's going on?"

"Nothing," Landry said.

"Just saying thanks for helping my pa fix his roof," Mooney said to Tobias, then turned back to Landry. "But I bet you're wondering why I didn't help him," Mooney went on. "I would have if I'd known he was having trouble with it."

Landry confessed the thought had crossed his mind, but he'd assumed the old man had no family close by.

"The old fool won't ask for help, and I usually don't hear about what he's been up to until he's up and done what he set out to do. Glad you were there to stop him this time."

"Happy to help," Landry said.

"My spread is just a mile or so outside town. I'd be much obliged if you'd let me know if you see him doing anything else stupid."

"Sure thing."

"Thanks." With a nod, he turned and walked out.

"So you've turned into a good Samaritan while I was gone, too?" Tobias asked as he exhaled a cloud of smoke. "Hell, boy, it's a good thing I came back before you turn into a saint."

Tobias and his two friends guffawed. Landry

wasn't amused. Picking up his beer, he drained the glass. "I have to go."

Before Tobias could respond, Landry stomped out into the night.

The sound of a boy's laughter drifting through the open parlor window of the orphanage drew Olivia's attention. With the baby she'd been rocking held snugly in her arms, she crossed and looked out.

Landry and Daniel were standing at the end of the front path. Her heart swelled. Daniel was grinning, and she realized it had been his laughter she'd heard. Since the picnic, Daniel had spoken a bit more, but no one had heard him laugh. Until now.

And it was all thanks to Landry.

The baby's eyes fluttered shut, but Olivia continued to gently sway back and forth as she watched Daniel and Landry outside.

As he'd promised, Landry had shown up a few hours ago. He'd been riding the horse he'd introduced as Chester, and he'd brought a smaller horse for Daniel. He'd assured her that the mare was docile and that provided Daniel could ride, he'd have no problem controlling her.

A while later, the two of them had trotted off across the fields behind the house in the direction of Miner's Pass, a trail that led to an abandoned silver mine.

As Olivia was settling the baby in the cradle near the front window, Daniel raced into the house, his eyes sparkling and his cheeks pink from the sun.

Olivia spun around and put a finger over her lips. "Shh. The baby's sleeping."

"Sorry," Daniel said, his voice as quiet as a child's could be without whispering. "Mr. Mitchell says he wants to talk to you."

Olivia's heart raced, and that now-familiar tingle whisked through her veins at the thought of speaking to him again. Did he know she'd be walking home at this time, or was it merely a coincidence that he and Daniel had happened to arrive back when they did? She knew she shouldn't, but she dared to hope he'd arranged to see her. "Can you please tell Mrs. Potts I'll be leaving now? She's upstairs with the girls."

Daniel nodded and raced off, his footsteps clomping on the wooden stairs.

Taking in a few calming breaths, Olivia retrieved her reticule and tied her bonnet on her head before stepping outside.

Landry heard the door open and smiled when he saw her coming down the steps.

"Afternoon, Olivia," he said.

"Afternoon, Landry. Daniel said you wanted to see me."

He nodded. "Thought I might walk you home if you're ready."

The dark expression in his eyes unnerved her. Was Landry concerned for her safety? Had he seen the man who'd attacked her? He didn't seem anxious to explain his motives, and if she was being completely honest, she didn't care. Whatever his reasons, she was happy he was there. She smiled up at him. "I'm ready."

As they strolled down the main street, several people greeted them as they passed. She noticed that a few even spoke to Landry. A twinge of excitement bubbled up inside her. Surely he had to see that people were starting to forget, or at least forgive.

"I'm not surprised you wanted to come back here," she said as they rounded the curve at the end of the street toward her house. "I love living here."

"You haven't lived here long, have you?"

She shook her head. "Almost two years."

"Where are you from?"

"Wyoming. Laramie, to be precise."

"You still have family there?"

"My mother lives there with her husband and his family," she replied. "I didn't have any brothers or sisters."

"What made you come to Rocky Ridge?"

She stopped when they reached her house. She stood for a moment, her glance taking in the gabled roof, the shutters, the long porch. She'd fallen in love with the house the first time she'd seen it, and now, with the rosebushes along the front of the house and the flowers lining the path to the porch, it was the home she'd always dreamed of.

"My grandfather," she said. "I didn't even know he existed until I received a letter from Brett Morgan after he died. He left me this house and an allowance so I'd never be forced to earn a living or to marry to survive."

"Floyd Evans was your grandfather?"

She nodded. "Did you know him?"

"He gave me a penny once not long after my ma died so I could buy candy at the mercantile," he said. "I never forgot that. I remember wishing he was my pa."

"From what I've heard, he was a kind and generous man." She'd forever be grateful to the man she'd never known for the gift he'd given her – not only a home and financial independence, but a new life with purpose and with people who cared about her.

"What about your folks? You were awful young to be going that far from home by yourself."

"My father was killed when I was thirteen. My mother remarried the next year. I became a burden to her and her new husband. When the letter came from his lawyer, Mr. Morgan, I do believe both my mother and my stepfather were glad to see me leave."

"I'm sure Miz Potts, for one, is happy you came and decided to stay."

She couldn't help asking. Looking up at him, she grinned. "Only Mrs. Potts?"

He didn't respond for what seemed like minutes but was likely only a second or two. Her breath caught in her throat. She hadn't realized until just that moment how important his answer was.

"I'm pretty sure other folks are happy you're here, too. Now I'd better get back to the livery. I have work to do."

Disappointment landed like a heavy weight. He wasn't happy she was here. "Of course. Thank you for walking me home," she said, keeping the tone of her voice as friendly as she could past the lump in her throat.

He turned, took a few steps, then stopped and turned back. "I'm glad you stayed, too," he said, then hurried away, leaving her with a smile pulling at her lips and a heart that had lightened considerably in the past few seconds.

Chapter Nine

The morning sun cast a golden glow behind the mountain peaks. Tobias had his arms draped over the corral fence outside the livery and one foot resting on the bottom rail the next morning while Landry carried buckets of water into the corral. "Ran into Emmett Farris this morning," Tobias said.

"What did he want?" Landry asked.

"Just making his lips flap. He's always been a jackass. Told me and my boys to get out of town."

Landry tipped one of the buckets to fill a trough with water. "What did you tell him?"

"Shouldn't have told him anything, but knowing him, he'd find some excuse to throw us in jail. So I told him we'll be gone in a couple of days."

That was news to Landry. Tobias hadn't said anything about when he was planning on leaving until now. "Where are you going?"

"Heading south. Soon." Tobias cast a sideways glance at his two friends leaning against the gate. "Just have to finish up some business."

Landry emptied the second bucket then exited the corral. "You never told me what kind of business you had here."

"Business that'll let us live like kings down

Mexico way."

"There's no business, no legal business anyway—"

Tobias straightened. "I don't need a lecture from you about right and wrong. In fact, I was hoping you'd want to come, too." He closed the gap between them and wrapped an arm around Landry's shoulder. "Be family again, just like old times."

Landry shrugged Tobias's arm off and moved away. He wanted his brother back, but he wanted the brother he'd been before, not the angry man who was standing in front of him now. "No, Tobias. I'm not interested."

"You don't even know what we've got in mind. Mexico—"

"The only way you can live like kings anywhere is with money. Money you don't have. And if you're going to rob somebody to get it, I don't want to know about it. I'm not going to Mexico. I'm staying here."

"Why? You think you're ever going to live in peace in this town? Or is it that woman you've got your eye on?"

"No. She has nothing to do with it," Landry lied.

"Good thing, because a woman like her ain't gonna get mixed up with jailbird like you. You're dumber than a stump if you think she will. There's nothing keeping you in this town. Folks here turned on you the day we hit the bank. You didn't do nothing wrong, but they turned on you anyway."

"I know that." He remembered that day like

it was yesterday.

"So what did you want to come back here for?"

He didn't know. Much as he'd tried, he'd never been able to come up with one solid reason why he'd been so determined to come back to Rocky Ridge and get his old life back. He'd only known it was what he needed to do.

And still, he was barely getting by, and until the past few days, whenever he wasn't working he spent all his time alone in a room that wasn't much bigger than a jail cell.

"Hear me out, kid—"

Landry shook his head. "I don't need to hear anything. I don't know what you're planning, but I don't want any part of it. And I wish you'd reconsider, too. You want it to be like old times? This isn't the way to make that happen."

"I'm gonna get paid for what they took from me, that's all."

"What's that?"

"Five years of my life," Tobias said. "Five years of filth, of food that wasn't even fit for pigs, of living with men who were no better than animals. No amount of money will give me back that five years, but at least I'll live in luxury for what time I've got left."

The bitterness in Tobias's voice shocked Landry. Everything Tobias said about prison was true, and even though the time he'd spent there had changed Landry, he was trying to put the whole experience behind him.

Tobias hadn't. And unless something drastic happened to make him see how wrong he was, he was going to end up right back behind bars.

"Listen to me," Tobias said. "You're never

going to get that life back again. You're a fool if you think you will."

"That might be, but I'm going to try. And I'd be real happy if you hung around, too."

Tobias shook his head. "We're going to be rich—"

"I told you I don't want to hear about it."

"You got something against having a nice house instead of a room, and a warm willing woman lying beside you instead of an empty bed?"

"No, but—"

"Just think about it. You and me could have a good life down in Mexico." Then he turned to his friends as he freed his horse's reins from the hitching post and mounted up. "Let's go."

Landry watched them ride off. Heaviness settled in his chest. He didn't know exactly what Tobias and his friends had planned, but he knew it wasn't going to end well. One way or another, he was going to lose his brother again. And this time it likely would be for good.

Cammie Todd was chatting with Lena McQuay on the boardwalk in front of the mercantile when Olivia happened by the next afternoon. "Are you off to knitting circle?" Cammie asked.

"I am," Olivia said. "Aren't you two coming?"

"Not today," she replied with a sigh. "My father needs me to help him in the store."

"Me either, I'm afraid," Lena put in with a loud sigh. "Mama and Papa are entertaining, and they're putting me on parade for all the unmarried men in their social circle. They've decided that, in their words, it's time I get married and learn my place."

Olivia's brows shot up. "Where exactly is your place?"

"Under the thumb of a man who'll rule my life."

"I think my place will forever be behind the counter of this store," Cammie complained. "I doubt being under a husband's thumb would be any worse than being under a father's."

"I wouldn't want to be under any man's," Olivia put in.

"That's because you have freedom to do as you like," Lena reminded her. "What I wouldn't give to trade places with you."

Olivia supposed she *was* lucky. She did have freedom, but she also had no one who cared about her, who'd look after her when she was sick, who'd worry if she disappeared.

"Well, we do have one evening of freedom, right?" Cammie asked. "You're both going to the dance, aren't you?"

Lena nodded, her bright red curls bouncing beside her ears. "I'm looking forward to it."

"Of course. I wouldn't miss it," Olivia said. The year before, when Olivia had first arrived in town, Priscilla had invited her to join the whole Morgan family at the annual dance. Even though she'd barely known anyone there, she'd thoroughly enjoyed herself. She expected to have an even better time this year now that she had friends.

"Wear the turquoise dress," Cammie said. "The one with the frill at the neck and the lace. I love that dress."

Olivia chuckled. It was one of her favorites. "For you, I will."

"Who knows? You might even find yourself a new beau there. The town is growing and a lot of people have settled here since last year."

"Thanks," she said with a laugh. "But I'm not interested in finding a beau."

"Sure didn't look that way when I saw you with Landry Mitchell the other day. You were all doe-eyed and looking at him as if he was the only man in the world."

Although the tone of Cammie's voice told Olivia she was teasing, she couldn't help the heat surging into her cheeks. "That's silly."

"Is it? Looks to me like you're pining for him whether you want to admit it or not."

"I am not."

Cammie's brows lifted.

"All right, maybe a little," Olivia said, "but he's not interested in me."

"Wear that turquoise dress and I guarantee you'll turn his head."

"He's not going to be there" Olivia said. "He told me he doesn't dance. And now that his brother is back in town—"

A voice from inside the mercantile cut her off. "Camelia? Where are you?"

Cammie sighed again. "Oh, I hate it when he calls me Camelia. Why couldn't I have a name like Jane or Ann?"

"I like your name," Olivia put in.

"I guarantee you wouldn't like it if it was yours."

The voice from inside called out again.

"Camelia? Where are you?"

"I'd better go in. What I wouldn't give to move far, far away from here. California, for instance. I'd love to see the ocean."

"Don't say that," Olivia admonished. "I'd miss you too much if you left. And besides, who else would tell me what to wear?"

Cammie chuckled. "Pay attention to me and you'll have Landry Mitchell eating out of your hand. See you at the dance."

Olivia watched as Cammie went inside the mercantile and closed the door behind her.

"I'd better hurry home, too, before Papa comes looking for me," Lena said. "I'll see you at the dance."

Lena rushed off, and Olivia continued on her way toward home. Perhaps she *would* wear the turquoise dress. It couldn't hurt.

Landry leaned against the corral fence outside the livery, listening to the music and voices from the dance drifting on the night air. The street outside the livery was usually deserted at this time of night, but tonight it was filled with wagons, buckboards and horses tied to the hitching posts.

The dance was in full swing on the main street, but closer to the other end of town. Lanterns had been hung on nails hammered into the porch posts along the boardwalks, illuminating an area that had been roped off for dancing and a dozen long tables loaded with food, lemonade and sarsaparilla.

Olivia would likely be there by now. She'd be dancing with the ranch hands who always came into town on Saturday nights. His gut burned at the thought of her in another man's arms.

He should stay away, far far away from her. She made him want things he couldn't have, made him think about a future – with neighbors, friends, a wife and a family. A future folks here weren't willing to give him.

The worst of it was, he wanted that future with Olivia beside him. Sometime during that afternoon he'd spent with her at the mill pond, he'd fallen in love with her. Or maybe he was already in love with her before then and just hadn't known it. Either way, by the time they rode home, he'd known he loved Olivia Harding. Loved her with every breath he took, with every cell in his body.

He couldn't offer her anything. He was a tainted man who'd tried to make amends, and even though he'd made progress, there were some folks in town who'd never let him make up for what had happened. He'd been in prison, and whether or not he was guilty of the crime he'd been tried and convicted for didn't matter.

He loved her enough that he'd never let her know. He couldn't ruin her life, no matter how much he wanted to be with her. She'd made a good life for herself here in Rocky Ridge. She had good friends, she was passionate about the work she did at the orphanage, and cared deeply about other less fortunate people.

Yeah, he thought, he should let her find herself a man who could give her the kind of life she deserved.

Even though he knew he should stay away, a few minutes later he was making his way down the street in the direction of the music.

If Olivia isn't there, he reasoned, I'll leave.

It seemed like every single person who lived in Rocky Ridge was there. Children raced around playing, babies slept nearby on blankets, elderly people sat on the sidelines tapping their feet to the music as the younger ones kicked up their heels to Pete Strickland's banjo playing *Buffalo Gals*.

Landry watched for a few minutes, his glance searching for Olivia. A shiver of unease snaked through him when he saw Tobias and his friends standing together near the front of the bank.

They had as much right as anybody else to attend the dance, but Landry couldn't help wondering if the three of them had an ulterior motive for being there. Whatever it was, it had nothing to do with him, so he dragged his glance away from them and scoured the street searching for Olivia.

He'd almost given up when he caught sight of her near one of the tables. She was talking to Camelia Todd, and as he watched, a man he didn't recognize approached. She smiled up at him, and then took his hand and disappeared into the crowd of dancers.

His gut twisted. He'd never known jealousy before, had never had deep enough feelings about one woman enough that he cared much who else she spent time with. It looked like there was a first time for everything.

"What are you doing here, Mitchell?"

Landry spun around. Emmett Farris was stomping toward him, his chest puffed out like a turkey ready for Thanksgiving.

"Just enjoying the music, deputy." Landry

couldn't resist emphasizing the word 'deputy'. He was pretty sure it stuck in Emmett's craw to be second in command, and the minute Zane Morgan quit his job as sheriff, Emmett would be right there ready to take over. And when that happened, Landry's life would be hell on earth here in Rocky Ridge.

Emmett's mouth twisted in a sneer. "We don't want the likes of you here."

"You mean *you* don't want me here."

"Same thing."

"Last time I checked, it's a free country. So why don't you go ..." He had to bite his tongue before he told Emmett exactly where to go and what to do when he got there.

"You might have hoodwinked the sheriff, but not me." Emmett's voice lowered. "Just watch your step, Mitchell. I'm keeping my eye on you."

"You mean watch my back," Landry muttered as Emmett stormed off.

Landry's gaze followed him until he disappeared into the crowd. A resigned sigh escaped him. Would it ever change? Would he ever be able to walk the streets, to go to a dance or church without people staring at him, or whispering about him behind their hands?

He wasn't wanted here. Emmett wasn't the only person in town who'd made that clear. He was just the most vocal about it. And all it took was a few people to make it impossible to live down his past.

But for tonight, he wasn't going to think about Emmett, or Mrs. Lundstrom, or any of the others in town who thought the way they did.

Tonight, all he wanted was to see Olivia.

Putting Emmett out of his mind, he turned to where he'd seen her a few minutes before. She was gone.

He swore. His rational brain told him it was likely better that way, but he couldn't stop the disappointment from wrapping around him.

Then suddenly, she was there, beside him. "I'm glad you came," she said, gazing up at him, her gold-brown eyes sparkling in the lamplight.

"Me too," he heard himself say. "You're looking real pretty tonight."

"Thank you." She smiled up at him, and his heart slammed into his ribs.

For a few long moments, they stood together silently, watching the dancers. Landry noticed Olivia's toe tapping to the tune Pete was playing and he smiled.

The music ended, and a few seconds later, started again. This time, it was slower. It was the excuse he needed to hold Olivia in his arms. He couldn't offer her a future, so a dance would have to be enough. At least he'd have that memory for the long, cold nights ahead when he lay in his bed alone.

"Like I said, I'm not much of a dancer, but I think I can handle a waltz. If you've got sturdy shoes on, that is."

Olivia grinned and fisted the skirt of the turquoise dress she'd worn, pulling it up just enough that he could see her shoes. "I'm willing to take the chance if you are."

Landry cupped her elbow and led her out onto the makeshift dance floor. She turned to face him and waited until his arm had circled her waist and he'd buried her small hand in his.

He had to concentrate ... one, two, three, one two, three ... which was darn near impossible when all his senses were warring with each other – her scent, the feel of her soft curves brushing against his chest, her whisper-soft breath in his ear.

If this was as close as he could get to loving her, he'd take it, and as long as she was willing to dance, he'd keep counting to three.

They danced for at least an hour, and Landry memorized every moment. Finally, she pulled away and splayed her hands on his chest. "Enough," she said, her cheeks pink, her eyes sparkling like gold in the lamplight.

Landry released her, even though he hated to let her out of his arms.

"I haven't danced like that in a long time. I've really enjoyed myself tonight."

"It's not over."

"As much as I'd love to stay, for me it is," she said. I should go home. Almira is feeling a little under the weather and I promised I'd go to the orphanage early in the morning to take care of getting breakfast for the children."

He nodded in understanding. "I enjoyed it, too."

"I ... would you mind walking me home?" she asked.

"I'd be happy to," he said, smiling down at her. Hell, he'd be happy to walk through fire for her.

All too soon, they reached Olivia's house. He held her elbow as they climbed the porch steps and stood in front of the closed door. "Would you like to come in?"

He'd like to go inside and never leave, but he shook his head. "That's not a good idea."

"You must be thirsty after all that dancing," she said. "I have lemonade and freshly-baked gingerbread."

"Thanks, but no." Lemonade wasn't going to quench the kind of thirst he had.

"Well, then, I suppose I should go inside," she said. Her soft voice made all reason disappear. He wasn't ready to leave, but he had no reason to stay.

"I suppose you should ..."

She turned and opened the door.

He couldn't do it, couldn't let her go inside "Olivia ..."

"Yes?" she asked, turning back to face him.

Even though his brain knew it was only going to make things worse for him in the long run, his body had other ideas.

He gently gripped her shoulders and drew her toward him, closing the gap between them. She looked up at him, her glance open, welcoming. He lowered his head, his mouth finding hers and brushing it against hers for a fraction of a second before he pressed his lips to hers, releasing all the love and hunger that had consumed him since the night they met.

He traced the seam of her lips with his tongue, and she opened to him, allowing him to taste her sweetness inside. Desire swept through him at the sound of her soft moan. She shifted in his embrace, and he lowered his arms, wrapping them around her waist, his hand splaying on her back. She reached up and wrapped her arms around his neck, entwining her fingers into his hair, her body yielding, molding to his as if they were two parts of one whole person.

Somewhere in that part of brain where he could still think, he knew he needed to stop before he lost all control.

He released her and took a step away, taking in ragged gulps of the night air.

In the moonlight, she glanced up at him, her eyes filled with raw desire. Her breaths were unsteady, as ragged as his. She raised her hand, trembling, to her lips, swollen from his kiss.

"I shouldn't have done that," he said, his voice shaky, "but I'm real glad I did. And I just want you to know, I wish things were different."

With her eyes boring into his, she took a step and rested her hand on his. "They don't have to be different."

Her heat surged through him, coiling tight in his belly. It took every ounce of willpower he could muster not to drag her back into his arms and bury himself in her softness. "They do, Olivia." He couldn't keep the sorrow out of his voice. "They do. And as much as I wish they could be different, we both know they won't ever be."

Chapter Ten

Olivia's eyes were gritty from fatigue and her body felt as if she was carrying a hundred pound sack as she trudged along down the street from the orphanage to the main street the next afternoon. She'd promised to go to Priscilla's for tea, even though was in no mood to be sociable.

She wasn't surprised. She'd gone early to the orphanage to prepare breakfast for the children, and since she hadn't slept more than a few minutes the night before, by the time she left after lunch, she was exhausted.

Landry's kiss – and his words – had affected her so profoundly she hadn't been able to put him out of her mind. He cared for her. He hadn't said it in so many words, but his meaning had been clear. And while she should be filled with joy and happiness that her feelings for him were returned, he'd made it quite clear there was no future for them together.

As she turned the corner to the main street, she saw Landry's brother and his friends leaning against the corral fence outside the livery. Landry was carrying two buckets of water to the trough inside.

Tobias said something, and Landry grinned,

then started to pour the water into the trough. Then he looked up, meeting her glance. She stopped, tempted to cross the street to speak to him, even though she really didn't want to have any contact with Tobias and his friends. Before she had time to make up her mind, Landry made the decision for her. He turned away and went back to pouring water into the trough.

Her heart filled with pain unlike any she'd ever known. "Oh, Landry," she whispered to herself. "I wish things were different, too."

Landry threw the thin blanket off and punched his pillow, then flopped his head back down. Night hadn't brought much relief from the heat of the day, and even the air drifting into the room through the open window didn't cool him much.

But it was Olivia that was keeping him awake.

He'd managed to avoid her ever since he'd kissed her after the dance, but he'd known it was only a matter of time before he saw her again. Rocky Ridge was a small town. It would be impossible for him to live his life there without running into her.

His stomach clenched, and his chest tightened. How was he supposed to spend his life here – seeing her, wanting her, loving her from a distance? How was he supposed watch her marry another man, knowing he'd be kissing, her, touching her, making love to her. Seeing her grow with another man's children inside her.

The answer was plain and simple. He

couldn't.

He had no choice now. He had to leave.

"What time is it, Miz Olivia?" Daniel asked as he rocked his small body in one of the chairs on the orphanage porch while Olivia swept the floor.

"A little after two," she replied. "Why?"

His small shoulders slumped and a frown creased his forehead. "'Cause Mr. Mitchell said he'd take me riding again. Miz Potts said I could go, and he said he'd come before two o'clock. But he didn't."

Olivia's heart stuttered. She hadn't seen Landry since their kiss after the dance. He'd come by to take Daniel riding three times since then, but both times, they'd avoided each other.

The last time, she'd forced herself to stay in the kitchen, knowing he was outside with Daniel. She'd heard Daniel tell him she was there, but he hadn't come inside to see her.

In a way, she was glad. Being with him, knowing there was no future for them, was too painful. At least if she didn't have to see his smile and remember the taste of his lips, she could try to pretend she was happy. Even so, he was never far from her thoughts no matter how busy she kept herself.

But one thing she did know, Landry wouldn't disappoint the boy if he had any other choice. "If he said he'd come, I'm sure he will. He's likely delayed because of his work. You must learn to be patient. Good things come to those who wait."

A proverb she should remember herself, she admitted. And it seemed waiting was all she could do – wait and hope something would persuade Landry to change his mind about them.

"Did you and Mr. Mitchell have a fight?"

Olivia started. "What?" Was the tension between them so obvious that even a child could see through the politeness?

"You didn't come talk to him when he was here yesterday," Daniel pointed out. "You used to talk to him a lot."

Yes, she thought, she used to enjoy talking to him, being with him. "It's fine, Daniel. Nothing for you to be concerned about." Olivia whisked the broom across the floor, sending dust and dirt flying off into the yard. "You may wait here for Mr. Mitchell, but be sure to let Mrs. Potts know when you're leaving."

Daniel nodded and turned away, his glance scanning the street, hope in his eyes.

Olivia went inside and put the broom away. She'd better hurry and leave before Landry arrived.

She wasn't fast enough. As she threw the door opened and hurried out, she collided with him as he was standing on the porch speaking with Daniel.

She couldn't prevent the squeak escaping her lips as she grabbed onto Landry's shirt to keep her balance. His arms snaked around her waist, tugging her into the muscled wall of his chest.

Her breath caught in her throat as she looked up and their gazes locked.

"Afternoon, Olivia," he said softly, holding her just a fraction of a second longer than necessary before releasing her.

She took a step back. "Landry."

For what seemed an interminable length of time, neither of them spoke.

"My ma and pa used to look like that," Daniel put in.

"Oh ..." Olivia had forgotten Daniel was there. "What do you mean?"

"Like they was mad at each other, but then I'd see them kissing when they thought I wasn't looking."

He grimaced, and Olivia couldn't help smiling. To an eight-year-old boy, grown-ups kissing would get a reaction not unlike eating Brussels sprouts.

"You ain't going to kiss each other, are you?"

Olivia would like nothing more than to be wrapped up in Landry's arms and to feel his lips on hers. Just the thought sent a tingling sensation through her to settle low inside.

"No, Daniel," Landry replied, but his eyes never left Olivia's face. "We're not going to be kissing. Ever."

Olivia heard Daniel sigh. "That's good. So can we go riding now?"

Landry nodded. "We sure can. Mount up and we'll be on our way."

Daniel ran off, and as Landry turned to follow him, Olivia reached out and rested her hand on Landry's forearm.

He stopped, faced her, his eyes mirroring her sadness and despair. "You're wrong about this, Landry," she said quietly. "I hope you realize it before it's too late."

He didn't answer, but spun around and bounded down the steps to join Daniel.

Landry sat on a bench in front of the livery

the next afternoon, watching as the stagecoach rolled down the street and came to a stop in front of the Wells Fargo office. Four guards rode in with the stage, rifles at the ready. A rifle leaned against the seat beside the driver, and another armed man sat beside him.

As Landry looked on, all the men except the driver dismounted. The driver handed a metal strongbox down to two of the men who carried it inside the office. One man waited at the door, watching the activity inside the office. The other two stood a few feet away, their eyes constantly sweeping the street for anyone suspicious.

So that's the mine payroll, Landry thought. He wasn't surprised the strongbox was being held in the Wells Fargo office rather than the bank. He'd heard the bank had been robbed three times while he was gone, and that Wells Fargo had recently installed a new safe in their office, one that was reported to be completely secure.

Landry leaned back against the livery wall and watched. A few minutes later, the men exited the stagecoach office. They stood together on the boardwalk for quite some time, then the driver climbed back onto his seat on the stage and flicked the reins.

Landry got up and waited for the stage to come down the street and stop at the livery. It was only then he caught a glimpse of Tobias and Uggie leaning casually against a post in front of The Lucky Shamrock. While they seemed to be uninterested in the stage's arrival, Landry suspected they were taking in every detail of what was going on around them.

A good citizen would go to the sheriff and tell him Tobias was up to something. But since he didn't know what or when, it wouldn't do the sheriff much good anyway.

He was glad he didn't know exactly what Tobias was planning. Tobias was still his brother, his own flesh and blood, the only family he had left. How could he turn him in?

Yeah, he thought, he was glad he didn't know.

"I don't know what to do." Olivia picked up the china cup with the floral pattern and took a sip of her tea while Priscilla bustled around her kitchen, sliding a batch of freshly baked molasses cookies onto a matching plate and putting them on the table between them.

Olivia sniffed appreciatively. The cookies were still hot to the touch, but she couldn't resist picking one up. She broke off a piece and popped it into her mouth.

"There's nothing you can do," Priscilla said, folding the towel she'd used to pull the tray out of the oven and setting it on the shelf beside the stove before sitting down opposite Olivia at the table. "If Landry's got it in his head that he'll never have the kind of life here that he thinks you should have, until that changes ... or he changes his mind about it ..."

Unfortunately, Priscilla was right. And Olivia had no choice but to accept it.

"What's even more worrisome now is that Tobias and his friends are back," Olivia said. "From what Landry told me, Tobias has always been such an influence on him. I'm so afraid he'll feel he has no choice but to go along with whatever Tobias suggests."

"Things are better for Landry now, though. People are starting to see he's not the villain they thought he was."

"They are improving, but people like Emmett Farris and Mrs. Lundstrom will see to it that his past is never forgotten. And now, with Tobias here ... " Her words trailed off.

"I can understand why you're concerned," Priscilla put in. "From what Zane tells me, Tobias was a good boy until his father died and he started running with James Uggers and Frank Gage."

"I don't like Tobias. Something about him makes the hair on the back of my neck stand up on end."

I agree," Priscilla said. "Both he and Landry were in prison by the time I came to town, so I didn't know them before. But Zane, his brother and his cousin grew up here. Zane told me that they were all friends until after Landry's mother passed. Tobias changed after that."

Olivia nodded. "Hopefully, Tobias will move on soon. The longer he's in town, the harder it will be for Landry to get his old life back."

"It will. Since Tobias's guilt was never in question, anyone associating with him will be judged the same way. Zane is concerned that Tobias is up to something, and that he'll try to convince Landry to join him."

As Olivia walked home later that afternoon, Priscilla's words ran through her mind again and again. She hadn't known Landry and Tobias when they were boys, but Landry himself had told her how close they'd been, how much he'd looked up to Tobias.

That closeness, that bond had been at the root of Landry ending up in prison. She couldn't help wondering how strong it was now.

Zane, Landry and Tobias had grown up together. Zane knew them better than most, and he was worried about Tobias's influence over Landry.

Olivia only hoped his concern was unfounded.

Clouds hid the moon, and the air was heavy with moisture. The tinny sound of music from the piano at The Lucky Shamrock carried in the silence of the deserted street, while faint light from inside cast shadows on the boardwalk.

Landry sat on the bench outside the livery trying to decide if he should wander down to the saloon for an hour or two, or go inside and try to sleep.

Movement in the shadows down the street caught his eye. He squinted, peering into the darkness. Was his imagination playing tricks on him?

No. There it was again. Three figures near the alley between the dressmaker's shop and the bank. And one of the figures was Tobias. He'd recognize the swagger in Tobias's step anywhere.

A few moments later, a faint glow of light appeared in the alley, then disappeared behind the building.

Landry's chest tightened as the realization of what his brother and his friends were about to do hit him. They were going to rob Wells Fargo. That was the business Tobias had been talking about.

The payroll for the Silver Dollar Mine was locked in the safe in the office, and the mine owner thought it was secure.

But they didn't know Uggie. He was one of the best safecrackers in the territory.

Landry bounded to his feet. He had to stop them! He had to stop Tobias before it was too late.

He hadn't been able to prevent his brother from getting involved with the wrong people five years before, but this time ... this time he would. One way or another, he had to make him see that this wasn't the answer.

Landry hurried across the street and down the alley where the three men had disappeared. He rounded the corner in time to see Gage working the lock on the back door.

Tobias swung around and drew his gun.

"It's me," Landry whispered.

Tobias slid his gun back in his holster. "Glad to see you've finally gotten some sense and you're coming with us."

"You can't do this, Tobias."

"You got something against living good, with money to burn, a soft bed and a warm woman beside you?" Tobias asked. "We'll have all that."

Landry shook his head. "You'll be on the run forever."

"Not once we get to Mexico."

Uggie moved to stand beside Tobias. "Your brother is a grown man, doesn't need a kid telling him what to do."

Tobias took a step closer to Landry, peered into his eyes. "If you're not here to join up, go home. The boys didn't want to split the money anyway—"

"No. I tried to stop you, to get there in time the last time, but I was too late ..."

"Was it worth the price you paid?"

"Every second of it, and I'll do it again if it'll stop this. You said you want it to be like old times. You and me. I want that, too. I want my brother back, but not like this ... like before ... like when we were boys. Do you remember, Tobias?"

"Yeah, I remember. I remember being hungry, and the beatings, and ..."

"We won't be hungry now, and Pa's gone. He can't hurt you anymore."

"Like I told you, it'll be like before once we get to Mexico."

Landry shook his head. "No. You won't get to Mexico. They'll hunt you down and either send you back to prison or kill you."

"You don't have much faith in me, do you?"

"Tobias, you've served your sentence. You're free now. You can start over." Landry took a step back then reached down, gripped the mother-of-pearl handle of his Colt and drew it out of his holster. He pointed it at Uggie and Gage.

Tobias's eyes widened. "What are you doing?" His eyes flitted from Landry to Uggie. Uggie's hands stilled on the door handle.

"I'm stopping you from making another mistake," he said, keeping his eye on Uggie and Gage. He knew it was possible that Tobias would jump him, but he also knew that deep down, his brother cared about him. "One way or another, I'm going to stop you from ruining your life."

Tobias had protected him all the time he was

growing up. His brother still had the scars on his back from getting between Landry and his father.

Now it was time for Landry to return the favor.

Prison had changed Tobias, but Landry was willing to bet some things hadn't changed. That he would never hurt Landry. "Either leave with me now or I'll shoot them both," he told Tobias.

"You gone crazy?" Tobias's voice grew louder, then lowered to a harsh whisper. "Put the gun away."

"Nope," Landry said, keeping his eyes on both men but directing his words to Tobias. "I will shoot them both."

"Kill us and you'll hang," Gage pointed out. "I don't think your woman will like watching you swing from the end of a rope."

Landry cast a glance at his brother. "What about you, Tobias? Will you like watching me die because of you?"

For several long seconds, their eyes locked. Finally, Tobias raked his hand through his shaggy hair. "You really think you can get your life back in this town?"

"I do," Landry said. "And I want my brother here with me."

Tobias's gaze shifted to Gage and Uggie.

"What's the matter with you, Tobias? You getting soft?" Gage rubbed his hand down the leg of his pants.

Tobias didn't answer.

"We're going to be rich," Uggie reminded him.

The lantern light flickered in the blackness.

Tobias's face was set in stone as his gaze shifted from one to the other, then back to Landry. "Okay," he said. "You win. If you're so dead set on staying here, I suppose I'll have to stay and keep an eye on you."

"The farm's still here, Tobias."

"It is?"

Landry nodded. "Remember, you always liked working the farm?"

"I did."

"Don't listen to him," Uggie put in. "We got plans. Big plans. And we'll be rich."

He turned to Uggie and Gage. "The kid needs me more than you do, so it looks like you boys are on your own."

Landry relaxed his guard and smiled at Tobias, repeating Tobias's words back to him. "I'm glad you're finally getting some sense."

Those few seconds were seconds too long to take his eyes off Gage. Before his brain even registered what was happening, Gage reached behind him and Landry caught a glint of metal before he felt a sudden jolt that knocked him off balance. It wasn't until he looked down and saw the dark stain spreading across his shirt that the reality sank in. He'd been shot.

There was no pain, only a cold chill washing over him as darkness clouded his vision. His legs crumpled, but he didn't have the strength to stop himself from falling. His head smashed against the wall of the bank, the pain barely registering in his brain. At the same time, he heard more shots.

Then blackness overcame him.

Chapter Eleven

Olivia started at the sudden crack of gunshots filling the air.

She'd been having supper with Cammie and Priscilla at the café while Zane attended to some business at the sheriff's office.

Now, Zane was escorting Olivia home after taking Cammie back to the apartment above the mercantile where she lived with her father.

As soon as the shots rang out, Zane spun around in the direction of the sound. His hand automatically reached for the Colt at his side. "Stay here," he ordered a moment before he began running down the street in the direction of the bank.

Olivia stood stock still for a moment, watching as doors suddenly opened and men filled the street.

"This way," a voice called out. Like a swarm of bees, the men hurried off in the direction of the livery stable.

Olivia's heart leapt into her throat. The livery.

Ignoring Zane's order to stay where she was, she joined the men and raced down the street.

Deputy Farris appeared at the entrance to the alley beside the bank. His gun was in his hand, but held down by his side.

The darkness made it impossible to see any activity past the deputy, but obviously something was happening.

"Homer!" The deputy pointed to a teenage boy. "Go get the doc. And make it fast."

"What's going on?" someone in the crowd called out. "Who got shot?"

"There's three of them back there. One of them's Mitchell."

Olivia heard the agonized cry, then realized it was coming from her own throat. Weaving her way through the crowd, she tried to rush past the deputy. He grabbed her elbow before she could get by. "Wait a minute, ma'am," he said, his grip tight on her arm. "It's not pretty back there. Not a sight for ladies."

Olivia tugged her arm from his grasp. "I'll be the judge of that."

Before he had a chance to say more, she hurried into the alley. A faint glow came from behind the bank, giving the alley enough light that she could see where she was going. Still, she needed to be careful where she stepped.

Her hand flew to her mouth when she saw the bodies lying on the ground behind the bank. Horrified, the blood drained from her face and she felt herself grow faint when she caught sight of Landry on the ground. His eyes were closed, and his skin beneath his tan was pale. Blood soaked the front of his shirt.

She didn't know what had happened, and at that moment, she didn't care. All she could think of was that the man she loved might be ... No!

She wouldn't even allow the word to enter her brain.

"Landry!" She fell to her knees and bent over him, her heart thundering in her chest. As she'd seen it done before, she held her hand to his mouth, letting out a sharp breath of relief when she felt a whisper of air touch her fingers. He was alive!

"Dear God," she prayed, taking his hand in hers, her glance never leaving his face. "Please don't take him from me. I've never loved a man until now, and I do love him with all my heart and soul. He may never love me back, but I can accept that if only you'll let him live."

She didn't know how long she knelt beside him, but she didn't move until Zane cupped her shoulders. "Doc Leonard's here, Olivia. Let him work."

Numb with fear, Olivia looked up into Zane's concerned eyes. She nodded and blindly let him help her to her feet and draw her away. Silently, she watched as the doctor examined him.

When he finally got to his feet, his expression was grave. "You men," he said, pointing to two men who'd followed Emmett down the alley. "Take him to my office, and be careful with him."

Without a word, the two men hurried to where Landry was lying in the dirt and picked him up. Olivia made a move to go with him, but the doctor rested his hand on her arm, stopping her. "I know you want to be with him," he said, his voice gentle, "but I can't work with you in the way. I'll send somebody for you as soon as I know something."

She nodded, her mind racing, her body numb as she watched the two men carry Landry away.

"The other men ..." Olivia turned to Zane once Landry, Doc Leonard and the two men were out of sight.

"Dead," Zane said. "Tobias Mitchell admitted to shooting them."

"But why?"

I haven't got the whole story yet, but it looks like it was self defense. One of them shot Landry and Tobias returned fire. Now, I'll get someone to walk you home so you can get some rest."

"That's all right, Zane," she replied. "I'm going to stay with Landry until he wakes up."

Zane shook his head. "Olivia, I'm sorry. I know you're fond of him, but the truth is, he likely won't wake up."

Olivia refused to accept that. Raising to her full height, she faced him squarely. "You're wrong, Zane," she said, her voice quivering with fear. "He *will* wake up."

For three days and nights, Olivia sat alongside Landry's bed in a small room in the doctor's office. Both Grace and her father had told her they'd done everything they could. Now it was up to him.

Hour after hour, she held his hand, sending her strength to him, willing him to come back to her. Yet he didn't move, didn't open his eyes.

She'd cried enough tears to fill the river, and her heart had shattered into tiny pieces at the thought he might still die. How would she ever survive it?

Olivia leaned back in the rocking chair Grace had brought into the room for her. Dusk was stealing the daylight, and she was exhausted. Still, she couldn't bring herself to leave any longer than it took to eat something and to take care of her personal business. She was sure that somehow, Landry knew she was there. She couldn't leave him to wake up and be alone.

Her hand rested on his, as it always did. She closed her eyes for a moment.

Then she felt it, a slight twitch of a finger.

Her eyes flew open and she leaned forward. His hand lay still under hers. Had she imagined it? Was it wishful thinking?

"Landry?" She spoke softly, little more than a whisper. "Can you hear me? Landry? If you can hear me, move your finger again. Please."

She moved her hand away from his. Her eyes locked on his hand. Time stood still, every second an agonizing wait. Then, when she was almost ready to accept the sensation had been a figment of her imagination, she saw his finger move.

Bounding to her feet, she bent over him and brushed her lips over his.

"Grace! Grace! Come quick!"

The door burst open and Grace rushed in. "What is it?"

"He moved, Grace," Olivia gushed, her heart racing with excitement. "He moved his finger."

Grace crossed to Landry's side and bent over him. She lifted his eyelids, held her fingers on his wrist and studied him for a few moments. He didn't move.

Turning to Olivia, she rested her hand on her arm. "I hope you're right, but I don't want you to get your hopes up. It might not have been a true movement. Sometimes—”

“It was,” Olivia interrupted. “I know it. I can feel it deep inside. He’s going to wake up soon.”

Grace smiled gently. “If he does, it’s because of you.” She moved to the doorway. “Call me if there are any other changes.”

Olivia nodded. “There will be. I’m sure of it.”

She had to believe that. She couldn’t bear to consider the alternative.

Why couldn’t he just die and get it over with? Pain unlike anything Landry had ever known consumed him, every breath sending jagged shards of agony through his chest. He was cold, too. So cold. Yet something warm was wrapped around his hand.

Images flashed through his mind – Olivia, Tobias, Daniel, the farm ... Over and over, they replayed, memories of fishing in the stream as a boy, of a willow tree near a pond, the glint of a gun, of Olivia’s eyes, filled with ... love.

She loved him. Deep in his soul, he knew that. She’d been willing to accept him, to love him, even though he didn’t deserve her. And he’d turned her away.

He should have told her he loved her. Should have let her love him. She was willing, and he should have given them both time to be together, to get married, to raise a family, to grow old together.

Now it was too late. If he didn’t die ... and right then dying was the best way he could think of to deal with the pain coursing through his body ... he’d be going back to prison.

Summoning every ounce of strength he could muster, he forced himself to open his eyes. He squinted into the dim light from a small lamp on a table in the corner of the room. The scent of cloves reached his nose, and the soft sound of someone breathing filled the silence.

Gingerly, he moved his head toward the sound. Through the hammering in his head, he saw Olivia in the rocking chair beside him. She was asleep, her long lashes resting against her pale skin, her lips slightly parted. He looked down and saw her hand on his.

It was her warmth he'd felt, her voice he'd heard. He tried to smile, but it took too much energy. He slept.

Olivia woke to find Landry watching her. She bounded out of the chair, sending it into a wild rocking motion that almost tipped it over. But she didn't care.

Landry was awake.

Her throat tightened and tears filled her eyes. Unheeding, she let them roll down her cheeks and drip off her chin. She moved her hand from his. "I'll get Grace."

Before she could move away, he wrapped his fingers around her wrist. "No. Wait."

"What is it?"

"I need to tell you ... I'm sorry."

Olivia perched on the edge of the chair. "Sorry for what?"

"I'll be going back to prison ... I'm sorry ..."

Her heart beating wildly, happiness filled her. She shook her head. "No." Her eyes filled with tears, but this time, they were tears of joy. "No prison."

Landry frowned. "I remember shots ... and I thought I heard loud voices ... Tobias?"

"He's fine. Uggie and Gage are dead. I'm sorry."

"Then what—"

"Tobias explained everything to the sheriff," she said. "How they'd planned to rob the bank but you came to stop them. When Gage shot you, Uggie went for his gun. Tobias shot them both."

Landry tried to sit up, but fell back against the pillow. "Where is he?"

"He's waiting for you at the farm."

"But—"

"They might have been planning to rob the bank, but they didn't. According to the sheriff, a man can't be arrested when no crime has been committed. He's free, and so are you."

Landry closed his eyes. Olivia was beginning to wonder if he'd fallen back to sleep when he opened them again.

"Landry, I have to tell you something ..."

His eyes searched her face. "What is it?"

She brushed the tears from her cheeks with the back of her hand. "I thought you were going to die ... and I hadn't told you ..."

His glance searched her face.

"Whether you like it or not, I love you. It doesn't matter if you love me back, but I needed to tell you—"

He smiled then, the first smile she'd seen from him in days. Her heart soared. "That's good ... because I love you too." He paused, struggling to take in a few breaths before he could go on. "It won't be easy being married to an ex-convict."

Olivia couldn't believe what she was hearing. "You do? You love me? And you want to marry me?"

He nodded. "Folks in town—"

"Are grateful you and Tobias prevented a robbery."

"But—"

"Let them believe it. There will always be those who think the worst, but the others far outnumber them." Olivia bent over and kissed him. It was a gentle kiss, but one filled with all the love in her heart. When she drew back, she glanced down into his dark eyes. "But if you want to, we can leave the livery and the farm to Tobias and go somewhere else, somewhere we can build a life together where no one knows you."

His eyes darkened. "No. We'll stay here. I don't want to spend my life worrying about the truth coming out, and I wouldn't expect you to live that way either. We can either build a house in town—"

"Did you forget I have a house?" she asked, unable to prevent herself from smiling at the thought of those rooms being filled with children.

"I did forget. You'd think Uggie shot me in the head instead of the stomach."

Olivia shuddered. "I'm grateful he did."

"You're glad he shot me?" he asked, his voice teasing.

"Glad he didn't aim for your head," she said with a laugh. "I don't think we'd be having this conversation if he had."

"You're right. Now about your house ... we can either live in yours or build another one here in town and I'll keep the livery, or we can raise our children on the farm. Your choice."

Olivia's tears started flowing again, but they were tears of happiness. "I'll be happy no matter where we live as long as we're together. But right now, you have to get better. I'll ask Grace if she has anything she can give you for your pain."

"What pain?" That twinkle in his eye she'd thought she'd never see again was back. "Come here," he said, taking her hand and drawing her closer until she was almost lying beside him on the bed. "You know what's the best medicine for anything?"

She shook her head.

"This." Cupping her head, he brought her lips down to his and kissed her until they were both breathless.

"Oh, my," she said when he finally released her. His breathing was ragged, and his dark eyes looked at her with so much love and desire her heart filled to overflowing.

"I'm pretty sure I'm going to need regular doses of that medicine for the rest of my life."

"I have a never-ending supply," she said, "and you look like you need another dose already."

"I do," he said gruffly. "I definitely do."

Epilogue

Guests filled the small church. Almira, the children, her friends … everyone who was important to her was there. Tobias stood at Landry's side, while many of his old friends sat near the back.

"I, Landry Mitchell, take you, Olivia Harding as my lawful wedded wife …" Olivia heard nothing but the sound of Landry's deep voice as he spoke his vow to her.

Now, almost a month after she'd almost lost him forever, she still found it hard to believe he was here, holding her hands, promising to love and honor her for the rest of his life.

Her heart was overflowing. She had almost everything she'd ever dreamed of – a man who loved her, a home, a community. There was only one thing missing, and she hoped that would be rectified in a few minutes.

"I now pronounce you husband and wife." The pastor's voice filled the silence. "You may kiss your bride."

Landry gathered her in his arms and kissed her soundly. Heat rushed into Olivia's cheeks at the depth of his kiss, but the guests seemed to enjoy it almost as much as she did.

The pastor waited until Landry had released her before he continued. Then, grinning, he turned to the guests gathered to celebrate their marriage. "I have one more duty to perform."

A low murmur of voices swept through the church. Olivia and Landry grinned at each other as the pastor stepped forward to join them. All three turned to face the guests. The pastor stood between them, then clasped Olivia's left hand in one of his and Landry's right hand in the other. "Daniel," he said, "can you come forward, please?"

Daniel looked around the church as if he expected the pastor to be speaking to someone else.

When nobody rose, he slid out of the pew and walked up the narrow aisle to the front of the church. He gave them a suspicious glance, his small mouth thinned.

"Daniel," the preacher said, "Mr. and Mrs. Mitchell would like you to become part of their new family. How would you feel about that?"

Silence filled the church, and for a few seconds, Olivia wondered if Daniel really understood what they were asking. As realization dawned, his eyes widened and a grin filled his small face. "You mean you'd be my ma and pa?"

Olivia and Landry nodded in unison. "We'd like to be, if that's what you'd like, too."

"Heck, yeah," Daniel shouted, then let out a whoop of joy. Then, suddenly remembering where he was, he clapped a hand over his mouth and gave the pastor a guilty look.

"It's quite all right," the pastor said with a smile, "this time."

The entire church broke out in applause.

"It seems Daniel approves of this union," the preacher said. With Olivia's hand still in his, he released Landry and placed one of Daniel's hands in Olivia's. He repeated the motion with Landry's. Then, smiling, he looked out over the guests. "Now then, it is my great pleasure to introduce, for the first time, the Mitchell family."

Olivia and Landry shared a look filled with hope for the future. Olivia was sure her heart was going to burst with joy and happiness. She was lucky enough to have found the one thing she'd always felt she was missing, and she'd treasure it forever.

A family filled with love.

Read on for a preview of

SUBSTITUTE BRIDE

by Margery Scott

Chapter One

Elizabeth Main's heartbeat stuttered as the postmaster handed the battered envelope to her twin sister, Sarah. It had been six long years, but she recognized the barely legible handwriting immediately.

Cole. Cole Berringer's scrawl.

"It's from Cole," she exclaimed, her insides abuzz with excitement. "Who is it addressed to?"

"Me, of course," Sarah said. "Although why he'd write to me now after all these years, I have no idea."

Elizabeth closed the door against a gust of rose-scented wind and the rattle of carriages passing on the cobblestone street. Her skirts swished on the polished wood floor as she followed Sarah into the drawing room.

Sarah crossed to her father's study and retrieved a silver letter opener from his desk, then strolled into the drawing room and sat daintily on a brocade chair beside the fireplace.

Elizabeth followed close behind, barely able to contain herself. She'd waited for this letter for six long years.

"Open it, Sarah," Elizabeth urged.

"Patience, Bee." The reprimand was softened by the smile on Sarah's face. "I haven't read it myself yet."

"I really wish you'd stop calling me Bee," Elizabeth said. "We're exactly the same age, and nicknames are for children. We're grown now." Sarah chuckled, the soft musical tone so unlike Elizabeth's own hearty laugh. "I'm sorry, sweet. I forget how much it bothers you that I'm four minutes older than you are. Will you forgive me?"

Elizabeth met Sarah's blue-eyed gaze and smiled. She'd never been able to stay angry with her twin for more than a minute or two. And she was much more interested in what Cole had written than she was in continuing her pique.

While Elizabeth paced the room, Sarah opened the envelope, then withdrew three pieces of paper and began to read.

Elizabeth watched the play of emotions on her sister's face. A tiny frown, a faint smile, her teeth worrying her bottom lip. Elizabeth couldn't stand it a minute longer. "Well? What does he say?"

Sarah looked up, her eyes wide. "He writes of all that's happened to him since the war, of his success as a rancher."

"A rancher?"

Elizabeth had been heartbroken when he hadn't come home after the war. A neighbor who'd returned a few months later had told her he'd gone to Colorado, but no one had heard anything about him since.

Sarah nodded. "Yes. He owns a cattle ranch, over ten thousand acres."

Elizabeth couldn't even imagine so much

space. Why, his ranch was likely larger than Summerton, where she and Sarah had lived until six months before when their parents died within weeks of each other.

"What else?" Elizabeth prodded.

"He wants me to come to Colorado. He wants me to marry him. Look." She held up a fistful of ten-dollar bills.

Elizabeth couldn't prevent the gasp that escaped her lips. Cole and Sarah? Married? If someone stabbed a dagger into her heart, it couldn't cause such pain, she was sure. In fact, she suspected her heart had stopped beating altogether. She could hardly bear to ask the question, but she heard herself voice the words. "Will you?"

The silence in the room was punctuated by the hourly chime of the grandfather clock in the corner. Elizabeth's throat grew so tight she feared she'd soon be unable to breathe.

Sarah smoothed the crumpled pages and folded them neatly, then slipped them back into the envelope. Before she had a chance to respond, the door burst open and an elderly woman rushed in. "Who was at the door?" she asked, fanning herself furiously against the July heat.

"The postman brought a letter from Cole, Aunt Meg," Elizabeth told her.

"Cole Berringer?"

The disdain in her aunt's voice surprised Elizabeth. What did she have against Clay?

Elizabeth nodded. "He wants Sarah to go to Colorado and marry him. He even sent money for her travel expenses."

"Good heavens." Aunt Meg's fan quivered like a hummingbird's wings. "That's ... that's preposterous ..."

"He's doing very well financially," Sarah put in.

"He's no better than that drunken father of his." Aunt Meg practically spit the words out. "I'm astounded at the nerve ... writing after all this time ... as if people had forgotten what happened and why he went off to war in the first place."

"I'm sure he's grown up by now," Elizabeth interrupted. "It was a long time ago." And not entirely his fault, she could have added, but decided sometimes silence really was golden.

"Hmmph. Nevertheless, you can't make a silk purse from a sow's ear." Her aunt had a proverb for every situation, and Elizabeth couldn't remember ever getting through a conversation without at least one being quoted. "Has anyone ever tried?" Elizabeth asked innocently.

"What ...?" Her aunt's face reddened.

"Maybe Sarah could turn Cole into a silk purse." Elizabeth couldn't imagine Cole being any different from how she remembered him - tall, strong, with eyes the color of slate and a tiny dimple in his chin that she'd teased him about for years. No, she couldn't picture him as a refined town gentleman, sipping tea with the ladies or dressed in a frock coat and derby.

Aunt Meg let out a bitter laugh. "The wilds of Colorado are the perfect place for the likes of him. He'd fit right in with the rest of the ruffians who headed west after the war."

Elizabeth was tempted to point out to her aunt that it was 'ruffians' like Cole, men who craved adventure and who were willing to risk their lives to explore new frontiers, who had discovered America in the first place. "I think he was very brave—" she began.

Aunt Meg scowled at Elizabeth. "Of course you do."

Elizabeth suspected this was part of the reason she'd fallen in love with Cole so long ago. She'd known it the first time she'd seen him that he was the only man she'd ever love. Of course, he'd been little more than a boy then, poised beside the Ring-the-Bell, his shirt sleeves rolled up, his sinewy forearms gripping the mallet, and a cocky grin on his face. In one smooth effortless arc, he'd swung. She'd watched as the mallet had hit the board at the bottom, sending a piece of metal flying up a tower. A moment later, the bell had rung. At that moment, she'd fallen in love, and even though her heart had been shattered when he'd begun courting Sarah, her love for him had grown stronger with every passing day.

And then he'd left. Gone to fight for the Union Army. She'd prayed every night for his safe return, and even though he hadn't come home when the fighting was over, at least he'd been alive.

"Elizabeth?"

Sarah's voice interrupted her reverie. "I wonder if there are shops in Colorado."

Elizabeth could have given a two-hour lecture on Colorado. She'd read everything available on western travel and settlement, as well as the tales in the dime novels she hid beneath her mattress.

Aunt Meg harrumphed. "The whole idea is ridiculous. Why, I've heard about the west - lawless, Indians who capture women and ... well, never mind ..."

Sarah smiled up at her aunt and tucked the letter into the pocket of her skirt. "Don't worry, Aunt Meg. I have no intention of going off to Colorado."

Elizabeth heard the sigh of relief escaping from her lips and guiltily slid a glance to her sister and aunt. Had they heard her?

"Good. At least you have the good sense to stay where people are civilized and you'll be able to marry a man of who'll be able to look after you properly and treat you like the lady you are." Aunt Meg closed her fan and turned away. "Now, let's forget all about this Colorado nonsense. Tea is ready, and we still have many plans to make for the ball next month."

"Eighty-seven, eighty-eight ..." Elizabeth stifled a yawn as she sat at her dressing table later that night and ran the mother-of-pearl hairbrush through her long auburn hair.

Suddenly, the door burst open. Sarah hurried in and let out a distressed sigh as she flopped down on the bed, her frilly chemise and pantaloons flapping.

Elizabeth turned from the mirror to face her sister. "What's wrong? Is Aunt Meg trying to marry you off to old Lucius Grant again?"

Sarah grimaced and gave an exaggerated shudder. "I don't understand why Aunt Meg is so insistent I marry him. Why not you? It's not as if he'd even know the difference."

"I don't understand it either, but I admit I'm glad I'm not the target of her matchmaking at the moment. After her attempts to marry me off to Edgar Whittington, only to discover he has a wife and children tucked away in the country ..."

"That was unfortunate for him, but providential for you," Sara put in.

"It was, and since then, Aunt Meg has allowed me time to recover from my broken heart." Elizabeth began to giggle, and within seconds, she and Sarah were lost in fit of laughter.

When they finally composed themselves, Sarah gave Elizabeth a stern look. "The problem is that since you've escaped her clutches for the moment, she's turned her attention to marrying me off. I'm almost tempted to marry Cole just to avoid Aunt Meg's matchmaking."

Elizabeth's throat tightened. Surely Sarah wasn't serious. She'd made it very clear earlier that she'd rather wither away as a spinster than live in the wilderness with savages.

"But even marriage to that fuddy-duddy couldn't convince me to go to Colorado. Cole has been out in the sun too long if he thinks I'd even consider his proposal," Sarah said, running her braid around her fingers.

"But you were sweethearts," Elizabeth said, as if she didn't need to remind Sarah of her relationship with Cole. "You must have loved him."

Sarah waved away Elizabeth's comment. "He loved me, and I must admit I was flattered by his attention. He was very handsome, after all. But love? Heavens, no. Can you imagine being married to a man like Cole and living on a cattle ranch in the middle of nowhere?"

Yes, Elizabeth thought, her mind wandering. She'd imagined just that for years. Well, not the living in Colorado part or the cattle ranch, but she had fantasized about being married to Cole every night after she said her prayers.

Now, she could add a ranch into her imaginings along with space, fresh air, land. Working beside him on his ranch, raising his children, building a life together. Her heart stuttered at the thought. If only Cole had loved her instead of Sarah. If only the letter had been for her ...

"I'm going to bed," she announced, slamming the brush on the silver tray on the dressing table.

Bounding up, she crossed the room, slipped out of her robe and draped it across the foot of the bed. Climbing in, she turned her back on her sister lest she see in her eyes the longing for something she'd never have. "Please blow out the candle before you leave," she muttered as she pulled the blanket over her shoulders and closed her eyes.

Hours later, Elizabeth's eyes sprang open. The house was silent, the fire had died, and faint moonlight filtered through the curtains at the window.

The idea had germinated somewhere in her subconscious as she slept. She and Sarah were twins. They'd spent many hours giggling about how they'd fooled not only their parents, but the servants, their tutors, their friends.

Why not Cole? Could she fool him, too? Her heart skittered inside her chest. It was a dangerous plan, one that could ruin her reputation and leave her homeless. Yet, excitement gnawed at her at the thought of becoming Cole's wife.

Sarah didn't love Cole, so Elizabeth's actions wouldn't affect her. Sarah would never leave Philadelphia. So why couldn't she take Sarah's place and make her own dreams come true?

There was no doubt in her mind that what she was considering was wrong. Yet if it made him happy to think she was the woman he loved, and she was married to the man she'd dreamed of for years, how could it really hurt anyone?

She'd loved Cole since the day she'd discovered the difference between boys and girls, and her prayers that he'd somehow discover he loved her, too, had gone unanswered. Now, this opportunity had presented itself, an opportunity to make her dreams come true.

Yes, it was deceitful, and she was sure her plan was a sin, but the temptation was too strong to resist.

She would go to Colorado. She would become Sarah. And she would marry the man she'd always loved.

About the Author:

Author of more than twenty novels, novellas and short stories in several genres, Margery spends as much time as possible traveling in search of the perfect settings for her books. When she's not writing, you can usually find her wielding a pair of knitting needles or a pool cue.

Originally from the Scottish lowlands, Margery now lives with her husband on a lake in Canada.

Sign up for Margery's newsletter to find out about new releases and appearances, take advantage of special promos, get exclusive content for newsletter subscribers only, and much more.

Newsletter:
www.margeryscott.com/newsletter

Website: www.margeryscott.com

Private readers group:
http://www.facebook.com/groups/margeryscott

Facebook:
www.facebook.com/authormargeryscott

Twitter: www.twitter.com/margeryscott

Email: margery@margeryscott.com